I0593148

CIRCLES OF SEPARATION

A SPIRITUAL FICTION SERIES

WALDMEER SERIES
BOOK 3

DONNA GODDARD

Second Edition 2023

Published by Donna Goddard

Victoria, Australia

Paperback ISBN: 978-0645729627

Large Print ISBN: 978-0645875553

Cover design by Donna Goddard

www.donnagoddard.com

CONTENTS

OUTER CIRCLE

IMPERFECT

BRICK WALL

ADJUSTMENTS

CHOOSE AGAIN

FELLOW TRAVELLERS

PART II
THE MIDDLE CIRCLE
Darnall

CURIOSITY SHOP

MAKE-OVERS AND MOVE-ONS

MAGIC MEN AND WOMEN

WINTER LIGHTS

PERSONAL BAROMETER

NARROW LANE

HANDSPUN

PROTECTION

IN THE AIR

PART III
THE INNER CIRCLE
Borderfirma Mountains

ODIN OF THE GREAT VALLEY

LOWLANDS

CONTRACT

CROSSING

SNAKES AND BITCHES

DOING OUR BEST

PROLOGUE
AMIRA'S NAMES

When Amira first appeared as a human in Waldmeer at the beginning of the series, she was not called Amira but Maria. She entered Earth via the compatible but injured sixteen-year-old body of Maria. It was only as Maria matured physically, emotionally, and spiritually that she was given her intended name of Amira.

In *Circles of Separation*, she is known by different names in different circles. In the Outer Circle, she is Vera. On Earth —the Middle Circle—she is Amira. In Borderfirma—the Inner Circle—she is known as Lady Faith.

PART I
THE OUTER CIRCLE

DREAM ON

FORK IN THE ROAD

CHAPTER 1
BIRD OF PREY

INTER-DIMENSIONAL

*O*n the way to the inter-dimensional Outer Circle:
Vera stood very still. She listened carefully to Mullum-Mullum. She did not want to miss the few words he was giving by way of instruction. In his customary style, Mullum-Mullum spoke in a meaningful but mysterious manner.

> *Think not you can return on the path that leads to the*
> *fork.*
> *Taken once, it disappears as the choice lies ahead.*
> *Both roads will lead to somewhere, but one will be to*
> *nowhere.*

It was Mullum-Mullum who first told Vera about the Inner Circle. She was not sure who told her to go there, but apparently, it was already decided.

She glanced up, realised Mullum-Mullum was walking into the forest, and quickly asked if he had more advice.

He stared at her with dramatic grey eyes. They were deep enough to carry part of the world's creation in them. Powerful eyes. One would be foolish to underestimate their owner. Yet, they were also peaceful and kind. They looked like water, as if they were connected to all the water—all the rivers, creeks, and lakes—in this vast land.

"Remember, Vera," said Mullum-Mullum, "by far, the most common reaction of those who get to the first circle, the Outer Circle, is to abandon the quest immediately. Be not deterred, and you will have won the initial, important battle."

Vera felt that Mullum-Mullum's words were simultaneously frightening and reassuring. She startled as Aquilla, Mullum-Mullum's wedge-tailed eagle, gave a high-pitched squawk indicating he was about to move. Aquilla's mission in life was to tail his master. He fulfilled his mission with devout single-mindedness.

Aquilla was not the only bird around Mullum-Mullum. Many birds followed him, and they appeared to have different tasks. Some came and went, relaying information from far and near. Some were busy with domestic duties, although Vera was not quite sure what those duties were. Others were happy little creatures whose sole purpose was spreading joy.

Mullum-Mullum was gone. Vera turned to pick up her bag. She pulled her coat tightly around her and headed down the road towards the far-distant fork. Although somewhat daunted by her task, she knew she was not alone. For one thing, a family of the cheery chirping birds had decided to keep her company. Mullum-Mullum's doing, no doubt.

They flitted about and sang their little songs proclaiming the world to be a wonderful, safe place.

They will be good company, thought Vera.

She reminded herself that Mullum-Mullum had one day, long since passed, made this same journey. He would not have sent her on it if it was too dangerous or if he felt she could not succeed. That lightened her load. The birds chattered more loudly and seemed to be agreeing with her summation.

CHAPTER 2
HAPPY DREAM

ON EARTH

In Waldmeer:

Amira woke with a start and sat up to try and reorient herself. She noticed the thin line of early morning sun pushing its way through the gap in the curtains. She guessed that it was about 6 a.m. The fairy wrens were darting across the window sill. The brilliant blue forehead of the male was just visible. The larger and noisier cockatoos were starting to call out but were not yet enthusiastic in their conversations.

These days, Amira often woke from her night wanderings with a clear memory of them. She recalled last night's conversation between her inter-dimensional self of the Outer Circle, Vera, and Mullum-Mullum.

Whether it was a relief or not to wake up from her travels depended on where she had been. Regardless, she did have another reason to be glad of waking up in her own bed.

She quietly lay back down and moved closer to the

heavily sleeping body next to hers. She breathed in Gabriel's smell. It was the sort of smell that comes from a contented male body. She loved it.

Anyone would love it, thought Amira. *But not anyone is here. I am here. So, I will love it for everyone.*

She smiled at her sense of humour, aware that it might not be humorous to other people. She had never told Gabriel how much she liked that smell. One day, she would —if he stayed long enough.

She slowly slid out of bed and reached for her clothes hanging over the bedpost. Gabriel rolled over and made a complaining noise. He was still asleep, but he could complain even in his sleep. It would be a few hours before he was ready to wake up. By that time, Amira would have done many household tasks and relished the quiet, special morning hours alone.

PASSING GABRIEL HIS BREAKFAST, Amira sat down with her morning tea. Gabriel worked afternoons and evenings, so his hours and eating/sleeping patterns were later than hers.

"Did you have any dreams last night?" asked Amira.

"No. Why? I never dream. Or else I don't remember any," said Gabriel.

Amira saw many people in her night travels that she recognised. They often did not have the same body type, gender or personality as in this domain, but they had the same energy field. That is how she recognised them. Almost always, the individuals were unaware of any other life but the one they knew on Earth. Of all the people she had seen, she had not even once seen Gabriel. She didn't know why.

"You dream up enough stuff for both of us," said Gabriel affectionately as he took his plate to the sink.

A few hours later, Gabriel put his cardigan and scarf on and said, "One of us needs to make money and seeing as no one else is offering, I have to go to work now."

"Oh, you love your job," replied Amira with a wave of her hand.

Six months ago, Gabriel had been offered a job teaching college art in a town about forty-five minutes away. It was a larger town than Waldmeer, and numerous Waldmeer residents travelled to it every day for work. Country people get used to driving long distances.

"At least the scenery is nice," said Gabriel, "and I'm not looking at the next car's backside like all the city people."

The job had precipitated Gabriel's decision to remain in Waldmeer rather than return to Eraldus. He still worked on his own art, but three days teaching at the College gave a steady and reliable income—a bonus to any artist.

He was initially reluctant to take the job, feeling that he might be somehow betraying himself as an artist. Still, he was realistic and decided he could take it without betraying anything. It was working well. He enjoyed his students. They adored him, and he valued that appreciation.

After a few months at the College, he even told Amira that his art had improved as a result of teaching. Generally, Gabriel was loving lots of things at the moment. He was happy. That made Amira happy.

He leaned over, kissed her on the lips, and said, "What did *you* dream about last night?" He pulled her closer. "Did you dream about me?"

Amira recalled where she had been last night. "No. I

dreamed..." She paused and said, "I dreamed of somewhere else."

Gabriel looked at her intently, stepped back slightly, and said, "Well, you are awake now and here. Just remember that, or one day you will dream yourself to another place altogether."

He opened the front door and readjusted his scarf creatively. Amira pondered that her scarf usually looked plain in comparison.

"You don't need to dream about anything," said Gabriel. "We have a happy dream right here."

BREAK UP

CHAPTER 3
GETTING ON WITH LIFE

Ide walked along the main street of Waldmeer with her nine-month-old baby in the pram. His name was Landon. He wasn't named after anyone, nor did his name have a special meaning. It was simply the only name that neither Ide nor Farkas said no to. Farkas wanted an "unusual, cool name" because he said he didn't want his son to be like everybody else. Something like Blaze, Hawk or Slate.

"A baby is not a fashion," Ide had replied. "A little boy grows into a man. He needs a name worthy of his future." She liked names from the Bible (Peter, David or Timothy) or other religious books. "If not from an important tradition," said Ide, "then a least a name which means something of value."

Landon means *long hill*. Nothing particularly inspirational about that. But by default, Landon it became—Lan-Lan as he was affectionately called.

The first months after Lan-Lan's birth were a happy time for Farkas, Ide, and Ide's teenage boy, Christopher. Everyone was positive, grateful, and hopeful. However, Farkas soon fell prey to the battle in his mind. He became increasingly withdrawn. Even though there was no longer a pregnancy bump to contend with, Ide and Farkas hadn't slept together since well before Lan-Lan was born. That was writing on the wall.

As Ide walked along the street this morning, she caught sight of Farkas a little way ahead. Hurrying to catch up, she didn't look to see what he was doing. However, she soon realised he was walking arm-in-arm with a woman. If he had been a different sort of man (the sort that is affectionate with numerous female friends), there might have been no suggestion of it being anything untoward, but Farkas was not like that. To add insult to injury, he wasn't even trying to hide it. More, the woman was Elise.

When Farkas first arrived in Waldmeer ten years ago, he had a brief relationship with Elise, who would have been about twenty. Not really a relationship, more of a temporary distraction from grief. After a long absence and numerous failed and belittling relationships, Elise decided to return to Waldmeer. She was more worldly-wise and street-wise, but every man she had given herself to so willingly and foolishly over the past decade had taken another part of her. Her skirts were too short, hair too big, lips too red, smile too heartbroken, and soul despairing.

Ide stared at Farkas. He sensed her presence behind him, turned, and stared back at her defiantly. He didn't bother to take his arm off Elise.

Bryan was in the chemist and watched them through the window, even though he felt he shouldn't. He didn't like Farkas. There was a twenty-year age gap between the two men. Bryan's partner, Teresa, and Ide were both forty. Farkas was ten years older, and Bryan ten years younger. However, the age difference wasn't the problem. Bryan thought Farkas's aloofness and competitive attitude towards other men was arrogant and destructive.

"I don't know how Ide ended up with Farkas," Bryan would say to Teresa. "She's so nice, and he's one of those good-looking dickheads."

"If that were true," Teresa would reply, "then Ide wouldn't be with him."

WHEN HE GOT HOME, Bryan told Teresa what he saw at the shops.

"That's not good," said Teresa. "Perhaps you are right."

She had an uneasy, worried feeling in her stomach, as with impending doom. It wasn't just about Ide and Farkas. She and Bryan had been having their own problems.

Around the time that Lan-Lan was born, Teresa and Bryan became engaged. It was an unexpected engagement. Bryan convinced Teresa to do so by telling her that it could be a long-term engagement until she felt ready to get married.

Over the last few months, he had become more insistent on knowing when they would be getting married. Teresa joked and smooched her way around the topic, but that was only going to work for so long.

"I know I said we could wait as long as you wanted," said Bryan later that day, "but I feel it is long enough. I want to get on with our lives."

He had enough confidence to ask for what he wanted without shame.

"We *are* getting on with our lives," replied Teresa. "Does it matter?"

"It matters to me," said Bryan.

At that moment, Teresa's teenage girls walked through the flat door full of conversation and complaints about their time in the city with their father.

Thank God, thought Teresa.

CHAPTER 4
IMPORTANT

"I don't know what to do," said Teresa to Amira the following morning in the bookshop. "I don't think I can put Bryan off any longer."

"Are you trying to put him off?" asked Amira.

"No," said Teresa. "That sounds terrible."

As it was Amira she was talking to, and she probably knew anyway, Teresa admitted, "I only said *yes* to keep him happy."

"I know," said Amira.

"He was happy, and so was I," said Teresa. "He said we could wait until I was ready. So if I was never ready, we wouldn't get married, right?"

Amira raised her eyebrows and said, "Was that Bryan's understanding of the situation?"

"If I wanted to get married, I would marry Bryan," said Teresa. "But I don't want to get married. I thought I might get used to the idea, but I haven't."

"What is it about marriage that you don't like?" asked Amira.

"It's the whole damn stupid thing," said Teresa passionately. "I look at friend's wedding photos and think, *Idiots.*"

Amira laughed.

"They spend a fortune on a dress that they will never wear again, for an event that takes a year of their life to plan, for family (half of whom they have issues with) and friends (most of whom will not withstand the test of time). And, anyway, weddings are boring. They are so self-centred. And when it is over, the couple has to recover from the stress of the whole thing, which probably caused numerous arguments. If it goes well, they try to hang onto the high of it like a drug, trying to relive it. But it can't be relived because it is supposed to be a non-repeated event."

Amira smiled. She wasn't at all bothered by Teresa's intensity. She was always pleased when people cared deeply enough about their lives and problems to struggle with any issue.

"As if couples can live *happily ever after,*" said Teresa. "People are not that happy, and neither are their relationships."

"You are older than Bryan," said Amira, "and you have already been married and divorced and have watched the lives and relationships of your peers."

After a few minutes, Teresa said introspectively, "I am terrified that if we get married, after a few years, Bryan will not want to be there anymore."

There was a noise outside. Teresa and Amira watched through the shop window as the surf life-savers yelled instructions to the kids they were training in the waves.

"Bryan is making marriage important as a positive event," said Amira. "You are making it important as a negative event."

"What do you mean?" asked Teresa. "Isn't it important?"

"The person is what is important," said Amira.

THAT EVENING, Bryan was back on the topic. He wanted to alleviate the mounting stress of the situation.

"Will you marry me or not?" he asked directly.

Teresa was resigned. Bryan knew the answer by her silence.

"It's alright," he said, "I know you tried your best. However, I must also respect my own feelings. I want to be in a relationship with someone who wants to be with me, only me, publicly committed and making a life together as a team. I need that."

They looked at each other and knew they had to let the other go.

CHAPTER 5
SHARED PRAYER

While Teresa and Amira talked in the bookshop that morning, Farkas returned home, if but briefly. Ide did her best to salvage the sinking ship, but Farkas had no remorse. The line had been crossed, and he was not backtracking. Ide knew he would not cope with her saying the relationship was over, so she said, barely loud enough for him to hear, "You need to say it's over."

Farkas looked hesitant and somewhat panicked, although one would wonder which part of him would not have anticipated this. He gathered himself and said with a smouldering viciousness, "I told you right from the start that I wasn't going to stay. What you made up in your head about me is your problem, not mine. I never had any intention of staying. Why would I?"

Ide was taken aback by the unwarranted ferocity of it all. However, for some reason, she heard a tiny voice between the raging, screaming voices in her mind. It may have been the desperation of the situation, the realisation that she may not get another chance to say anything to him again.

"Before you go," said Ide, "I want you to know something."

Farkas prepared for what he thought would be a scathing comment about his character or lack thereof.

"I want you to know," continued Ide, "that my intention has never been and never would be to hurt you."

Farkas looked unsure of what to do or say next. He decided to walk out of the house defiantly. *Who* he thought he was defying was unclear. Seeing that he had a missed call from Elise, he opened his phone. He didn't return the call. He blocked her number, put his phone back in his pocket, and headed out of town.

THAT EVENING, Farkas tossed and turned, vainly trying to go to sleep.

Just get through tonight, he told himself. *It's the hardest one. Every one after this one will be easier. Tomorrow morning, the sun will come up, it will be a new day, and there will be hope for something better.*

Three other people (Ide, Teresa, and Bryan) shared the same prayer, with the same desperation and sincerity, that same night.

CHAPTER 6
LAN-LAN

The next day, Teresa, Ide, and Amira sat together in the cafe. Lan-Lan was on the floor of the play area next to them. He was fascinated with the antics of the children around him. As he needed no attention, at the moment, the three women were free to talk. There was more crying than talking.

On the family farm, Bryan cried too. He cried when he was way down the paddock where no one could see him. The cows were a nonjudgmental crew.

Farkas didn't cry much. His tears stayed inside him. They came out as anxiety.

Lan-Lan laughed at the other children. Unlike everyone else, he was in the best of moods with not a care in the world. The women smiled and felt a little better.

"Who's going to look after Lan-Lan when you are at work?" asked Amira.

"I don't know," answered Ide. "I'm not sure when or if Farkas will be back to help with him."

"I will help you until he has sorted himself out," said Amira.

"I can't ask you to do that," said Ide. "You have your own work."

"You *can* ask me," said Amira emphatically, picking up the smiling, cooing baby. "There are always people needing help. My work can wait. Babies can't."

On the way out, Teresa quietly said to Amira, "I can think of someone who might not be as enthusiastic as you about your having Landon."

'Yes," admitted Amira. "Gabriel may not be so thrilled with the idea." She added with a smile, "Perhaps I won't tell him whose baby it is."

Teresa rolled her eyes and said, "That can hardly end well."

LONG HILL

CHAPTER 7
TWO VIEWS

ON EARTH

I n Waldmeer:
I hope I don't go anywhere tonight, thought Amira as she fell into bed. She felt so tired after all the break-up drama with her friends.

INTER-DIMENSIONAL

IN THE INTER-DIMENSIONAL LONG HILL, on the way to the Outer Circle:
Vera was aware of Aquilla's coming and going as she walked along. She assumed he was keeping an eye on her and then returning to Mullum-Mullum. Wedge-tailed eagles are predominantly aerial creatures, soaring for hours on end without beating their wings. Their eyesight is extraordinary and extends into ultraviolet light bands.

All of a sudden, Aquilla dived towards Vera with remarkable speed. The presence of a diving wedge-tailed eagle causes panic among other birds. They started squawking and scattered in all directions. Several brave magpies made futile attempts to look aggressive, flying towards the eagle and then darting away again. Aquilla ignored them all as if it was a big to-do about nothing. He roared past Vera, dropping a note on the ground ahead of her.

I am sending you a guide.
He rules the land you are currently entering.
It consists of many gentle hills which slowly ascend to the Outer Circle.
From a distance, the land looks like one long hill, although it is made of many smaller ones.
Thus, it is known as Long Hill.
The guide's name is Lan-Lan.

The note was from Mullum-Mullum. Lan-Lan appeared shortly after. Vera heard him more than saw him, as he was semi-transparent.

"Each of my hills has two views," said Lan-Lan. "You will see the views at the top of each hill. One is bad. One is good. If you need me, call."

CHAPTER 8
CHANGING THE OUTLOOK

INTER-DIMENSIONAL

Vera reached the summit of the first hill, and sure enough, a view was in front of her. It was very pleasant, full of interesting activity—obviously the good view. However, no sooner had Vera surmised this than it began changing form. The enchanting images formed into dark, menacing ones.

What I assumed to be the good view is not good at all, thought Vera. *It is a mask for the bad view. But where is the good view, then?*

Not wanting to travel forward into the bad view, she called Lan-Lan.

"Having discerned which is the unwanted bad view," said Lan-Lan, "you must now un-see it."

"It seems very real," said Vera.

Lan-Lan slowly walked towards Vera (or glided, as translucent people tend to do), passed his hand over her head, and closed her eyes lightly with his palm.

When Vera opened her eyes and looked out, the view had completely changed into a serene scene of charming hills, shimmering rivers, grazing animals, and tiny towns. The whole scene was caressed with soft sunlight—the true good view.

"This is the natural and true state of Long Hill," said Lan-Lan. "Every time you get distracted, remember this."

As Vera progressed, she found that the unpleasant views, which had previously been very general, were becoming more specific.

"Each one must be corrected," said Lan-Lan.

Again, Lan-Lan passed his hand over Vera, saying, "What I see is not the truth. Above all, I wish to see."

It took Vera quite a while, but eventually, each one changed, and she became certain and calm.

She reached the top of Long Hill with a tender assurance inside her.

~

ON EARTH

Back in Waldmeer:

Amira felt well-rested, at ease, and peaceful when she woke up. Later that day, she looked after Lan-Lan while Ide was at work. She kept peering into Lan-Lan's eyes, searching for something—some recognition, evidence of more. Nothing. She couldn't find anything.

"I had to go to the bank today to see what I could do about the mortgage," said Ide that evening when she picked up Lan-Lan. "I can't pay it on my own."

"No, of course not," said Amira. "What did they say?"

"They said that money had been deposited into the account today," said Ide, "and everything is fine."

"Really?" said Amira. "That's great."

"Yes," said Ide. Her face relaxed. Some of the trauma was starting to go. "I guess Farkas hasn't gone as far away as I thought."

As Amira passed Lan-Lan back to Ide, she thought, *There is something unusual about Lan-Lan. He is always happy.*

It was such a pleasant trait that it almost went unnoticed. He hardly cried, didn't get sick, slept well, and was undisturbed by other people's emotions. He came with happiness inside him, and he was already sharing it with the world.

CHAPTER 9
NEXT BEST THING

Although Gabriel and Bryan did not get along well with Farkas, they got along well with each other. Both men's preference was for lack of conflict. However, if push came to shove, both were prepared to stand their ground.

They were not dissimilar in nature, although Gabriel was more creative and free-thinking, and his life experience was broader. If Bryan made a comment that sounded too country-hick for Gabriel's liking, Gabriel would make a joke about it.

Bryan may have been more conventional (boring) than Gabriel, but he was also more mature. For one thing, he didn't laugh at other people's expense. Depending on the company Gabriel kept, he could and did. Also, if Gabriel was having one of his downward spirals, he could become angry for whole stretches of time. Bryan didn't tend to do that. He tried to fix up his problems in a relatively decisive and constructive way.

One of those problems was, of course, Teresa. That

particular problem was not succumbing to Bryan's normal problem-solving methods. Although Bryan and Teresa had broken up, he had found a reason to come into town from the farm every day this week. He would get coffee, take one to Teresa, and stay at the bookshop talking.

Deciding that it wasn't sensible to keep doing that, Bryan asked Gabriel if he wanted to catch up for coffee instead. After some guy-type small talk, Gabriel asked Bryan how he was doing.

"Not too bad," said Bryan. "We made our decision. We have to get on with it now."

Gabriel was as little convinced by that response as Bryan was.

"Yeah, sure, man," said Gabriel. "Just gotta get on. Plenty of fish in the ocean."

Bryan didn't bother to smile.

Searching for something to say that would help, Gabriel added, "Was there a particular problem?"

"We saw the future differently. That's all," said Bryan.

Although friendly to everyone, Bryan was one of those men who only trusted his woman with important personal information. As he didn't have that woman anymore, he suddenly decided that Gabriel was the next best thing.

"I don't know, dude," said Bryan. "It was going great, but then I realised Teresa didn't want to get married, and it all fell apart."

Gabriel nodded and said, "I suppose that was different to what you had in mind."

"Yeah," said Bryan. "It was."

"I'm not one to give relationship advice," said Gabriel, "but does it matter that much? Is it worth losing her over? Isn't it more important to look at the person sleeping next to you and think, *This is the person I want to be with, problems and all?*"

Bryan nodded and said honestly, "I guess it somehow seems safer if the person marries us."

Gabriel laughed and said, "I don't know how safe it is. These days, if people don't want to stay, they don't."

"I don't want the person I love to feel like a prisoner," said Bryan. "I just don't want to get hurt myself."

"And you don't want to be the prisoner," added Gabriel. "At least, I don't."

SOMEONE LOVES YOU

CHAPTER 10
EMPERORS AND KINGDOMS

Since Gabriel had been living in Waldmeer, he had not seen Thomas. They no longer had their styling-shopping sessions as Gabriel was no longer in the city. In Waldmeer, their circles didn't intersect. Thomas's world consisted almost entirely of school-related people and events. Kathleen, Thomas's ex-girlfriend, was the only person he saw who did not belong to school.

This morning, Gabriel saw Thomas walking out of the supermarket. At least, he thought it was Thomas, but he had to do a double-take to be sure. Thomas looked like he had aged five years in six months and had unfortunately reverted to his old man's dress code which aged him a further ten years.

"Hey, buddy," said Gabriel cheerfully.

Thomas instantly recognised the voice behind him because few people talked to him in that tone. It wasn't that the tone was special. The point was that it wasn't. When one lives as emperor of one's kingdom, one is generally seen as a master or enemy. Both engender respect but not the relaxed, open tone one has towards an equal.

Thomas was in a hurry but stopped and said, "Good to see you. Are you visiting Waldmeer?"

"No, I live here now," said Gabriel. "With Amira."

Thomas looked surprised. Somebody usually told him the gossip, but he guessed that his regular informants must not have been interested in Amira.

"You're a lucky man," said Thomas.

Gabriel was about to say something but decided against it.

"How are you?" he asked.

"Fantastic," said Thomas. "Couldn't be better."

"Yeah?" said Gabriel. *Men are stupid,* he thought.

"Actually," said Thomas, "I have been sick, and I can't seem to shake it. I'm a little down in the dumps."

"Sorry to hear that," said Gabriel.

"Today," said Thomas, "I am signing a new five-year contract as Principal of Waldmeer State Secondary School. They still must want this old badger."

"Of course they do," said Gabriel. "You are the best thing that has happened to that school. That's what Amira tells me, anyway."

"Thanks," said Thomas with a restrained smile. "I hope all my years have counted for something."

Not one to drum up business for Amira, Gabriel nevertheless said, "Why don't you go see Amira? She has been looking after a friend's baby lately, but I don't think she has him this morning."

Thomas shook his head. He was too busy. Or scared.

CHAPTER 11
COURAGE

On the way back to school, Thomas's car turned left instead of right, and he ended up outside Amira's house. As much as he didn't like to admit it, he was a little nervous of Amira. She could be harsh.

"How lovely to see you," said Amira as she opened the door.

Butter wouldn't melt in her mouth.

"I don't have long," said Thomas, "but I thought I would drop in."

Amira knew by the look of him that he wasn't well. She made him a cup of tea, and they sat on the back verandah listening to the forest sounds that were a mere few streets away. The forest was an ever-present backdrop to life in Waldmeer.

"I can't say that I'm unhappy," said Thomas, "but I can't say that I'm happy either." He listened to one of the laughing kookaburras high in a nearby gum tree. "Maybe, I am unhappy. Or, at least, I am more unhappy than happy."

"Perhaps, you need a change," said Amira.

"Nothing will be changing," said Thomas defensively. "I'm signing another contract today."

Amira sensed that this was the immediate and precipitating problem. However, she could also see that Thomas wasn't aware of it yet.

"Sometimes," she said, "things need to change, and if we don't listen, we will miss out on what is next."

"Yes," replied Thomas without stopping to think, "I always tell my staff and students that brave people are not fear-free, but they don't let their fear stop them from progressing."

Amira let the awkward silence sit for a while and then said, "Remember, someone loves you."

She pointed towards the sky. She could have been pointing anywhere. Perhaps, everywhere.

CHAPTER 12
SO MUCH MORE

One of the school's board members said to Thomas who had pen in hand, "Several of us have been in this with you since the beginning. We will probably be in it together till the day we die."

He slapped Thomas on the shoulder and slid the contract towards him.

Till the day we die, thought Thomas.

He looked at the board member. He saw an old man. A kind-hearted but fumbling, weak, delusional old man. He looked around at the other board members. Some were younger and fresher, but the bulk were his age and had been there as long. They all seemed so old. Thomas dared not look at himself in the large mirror on the boardroom wall.

My God, he thought, *we are all dying and hanging on to school as if we have nothing else.*

He remembered that yesterday morning, he had told a group of stressed and anxious final-year students that their identity was not dependent on their exam results or anything else that they may happen to do in life. "You are so much more," he told the group with the conviction of an evangelist.

He also remembered a twelve-year-old boy he had spoken to that morning. The boy had arrived in Waldmeer a month ago and was struggling with anxiety and some low-level bullying from the local lads who were a bit too full of energy and themselves.

Thomas knelt before the shaking boy and said as quietly as possible so as not to frighten him, "Right now, you are scared, aren't you?" The boy nodded. "I promise you, if you keep going and believe that you have something to give, it will all get better."

The idea made the boy stop thinking about how alone and afraid he was. He started to wonder what he had to give.

"Now, don't you forget," said Thomas as the boy was leaving, "you can come to me any time you need to. If the ladies in the office tell you that I am too busy, you are to say that you have special authority from me to get a time slot."

The boy practically skipped out of the room.

Thomas turned to the board members, slowly and deliberately put the pen on the large polished table, and pushed the unsigned contract back to his colleague.

"Ladies and gentlemen," he said, "it is time. There is more for me. So much more."

PLAY NICE

CHAPTER 13
IN THIS TOGETHER

Since leaving Ide, Farkas had been staying in a motel ten minutes outside Waldmeer. Contrary to his initial hypothesis that every night would be easier after the first night, every night was getting more depressing.

He decided to take a drive into the Leleks. Maybe the forest would help. He had to pass back through Waldmeer and stopped for coffee. The coffee shop was next door to the Opportunity Shop. On seeing it, Farkas went back to his car to get several bags that had been travelling with him for months.

The drop-off area was locked, so he had to take the bags into the shop. Someone was crying. He didn't want to stay, but something about the sadness in the unguarded voice made him stand still. He coughed to make his presence known. The crying instantly stopped, and a lady appeared from the back room.

"I'm dropping these bags off. Okay?" said Farkas turning to leave.

"Wait a minute," said Amelia, the shop assistant. "We have to check them to make sure you are not giving us rubbish."

Farkas groaned. Amelia must have been the slowest shop assistant in the world. He would have left, but Amelia started crying again as she slowly, painstakingly, checked his bags.

"Are you alright?" asked Farkas.

Amelia looked up and saw a kindness in Farkas's eyes.

"No, I'm not alright at all. I just don't understand why people have to be so mean."

"What did they do?" asked Farkas.

"My tennis group doesn't want me anymore," said Amelia.

The look on Farkas's face would have let her know that he hardly thought that was the end of the world, but Amelia was too busy being upset to notice.

"What did they say?" asked Farkas.

"That I only think about myself," said Amelia. "Imagine saying such a thing."

"Imagine," said Farkas.

"They say that I am the weakest link. I most certainly am not. I can surely play better than several of the other ladies."

Pathetic, thought Farkas.

He looked at Amelia. She was about sixty. Even though there would only be ten years between him and Amelia, the difference in the state of their bodies was more like thirty years. She was overweight and had the coordination, or lack thereof, of a woman who had done little physical exercise her entire life. It was difficult to visualise her running around a court, let alone getting a ball where she wanted it.

If she is not the worst, then the rest must be pretty awful, Farkas thought.

"I'm sure you can play better than some," said Farkas.

"Thank you," said Amelia looking with interest at the stranger. "What did you say your name was?"

"I didn't. It's Farkas."

"I wish they had your good sense."

"Who told you to leave the group?" asked Farkas.

"My friend, Verloren," said Amelia. "No one said she is the boss of the group, but all the ladies do what she says. I don't know why."

"I know her," said Farkas, who had known her for years. "What did she say, exactly?"

"She said that I flirt with the coach and try to own him," said Amelia.

"Do you?" asked Farkas.

"No, I most definitely do not," said Amelia.

"What else did she say?" asked Farkas.

"She said I am selfish and nasty and always want the best spot," said Amelia. "How could she say that?"

Farkas shrugged and passed Amelia a tissue. She took it and held onto his hand as she cried. He didn't pull away.

She doesn't mean any harm, he thought. *Actually, she probably does, but it's all so pathetic.*

Eventually, Farkas said that he had to go. "You tell Verloren I said she has to let you back in."

"She won't listen," said Amelia.

"She will listen," said Farkas as he walked towards the door. "No more flirting, and be nicer to the other ladies. They are your friends, and you are all in it together. You are not the only one who loves tennis. I'm sure they all love it as much as you. Play nice."

What a gentleman, thought Amelia. *Maybe, I'll ask him if he wants to join our tennis group?*

With that thought, she brightened up and picked up the phone to call Verloren to tell her about her new friend.

CHAPTER 14
NUMBER FORTY-FIVE

In the Leleks (the forest behind Waldmeer):

Feeling less despairing, Farkas drove along the winding dirt track into the Leleks. He had a sense of inevitability as he crossed the walking bridge into Erdo's territory. Although this was his third time crossing that bridge, he had never met Erdo. Erdo didn't say anything as he stood next to the lake. He indicated for Farkas to follow him.

They walked thirty minutes into the forest and came to an old cottage that Farkas assumed was Erdo's home. Beyond it was a working farm—rows of vegetables, a small orchard, hens, and some crops in the distance.

Strange, thought Farkas. *Over all these years, Amira never mentioned that Erdo had a fully functioning farm.*

He noticed the number forty-five on the front wall of the house. He wondered what it was forty-five of. There was no street or road of any kind. There were certainly no other houses. Underneath the number was a rustic wicker basket with long, thin branches resting hocus-pocus inside. To break the tension, he joked that the basket looked like something for witches' brooms.

"Don't be ridiculous," replied Erdo. "They park out the back."

Once inside, he said, "I sleep upstairs. Your room is here at the back of the house."

Although simple, the cottage was very homely. A sense of safety and contentment seemed to emanate from its walls.

"You will be helping with the farm jobs, bright and early," said Erdo.

Farkas was not a farm-type. Although very healthy, his skin was pale, and he was thin. He didn't have the robust body type of a farmer. Nor the appetite. He usually wasn't that interested in food. Add to that a fast metabolism, and there would never be excess weight on him.

One day, in the first week, Farkas did try and leave. He headed in the direction of the bridge. However, after an hour, he ended up back at the farm. He had walked in a circle, although he wasn't sure how.

After that, he settled into farm life's steady, predictable nature. Over the next few weeks, the paleness left, his appetite grew, his muscles felt like they were working purposefully, the thoughts that tended to preoccupy his mind lessened, and he started to feel and look different.

One evening, next to the fire, Erdo asked Farkas if he had a family.

"I have a son," answered Farkas.

"Where is he?" asked Erdo.

"With his mother," replied Farkas.

"Do you help with him?" asked Erdo.

Farkas glared at Erdo and said, "Of course I do! He's my

child. I pay child support through the mortgage account. I'm not a jerk."

Unperturbed, Erdo said, "I didn't think you were."

He turned to the black cat lying at the foot of the wood stove and asked, "Do you think Farkas is a jerk, Francis?"

Francis looked contemptuously at both of them, raised her bottom in the air, and walked off disdainfully.

"Isn't she a sweetheart?" said Erdo seriously.

Farkas thought she belonged with the witches and their brooms.

A FEW DAYS LATER, Ide got a letter from Farkas. It had no stamp, so Ide assumed it was hand-delivered. All it said was that he hoped she and Lan-Lan were okay and that he was working in the forest. The return address was No. 45, The Leleks. Ide asked Amira if she knew where that was, but she had no idea.

"So long as *he* knows where he is," said Amira, "that's the important thing."

OUTER CIRCLE

CHAPTER 15
SCAMMERS AND SCANNERS

INTER-DIMENSIONAL

*I*n Long Hill, at the entrance of the inter-dimensional Outer Circle:

"When you enter the Outer Circle," said Lan-Lan to Vera, "the most pressing problem is recall. On moving into its atmosphere, you will forget who you are and why you are there."

"If I cannot remember who I am, I will be very vulnerable," said Vera as she backed away from the entrance at the top of Long Hill.

"Don't worry," said Lan-Lan. "The loss of memory is only partial. If you can grasp onto some of it, its return will be hastened."

He stepped through the archway into the Outer Circle, saying, "I will be with you."

Vera glanced backwards to Long Hill, but instead of being inviting, it looked misty and impenetrable. She recalled Mullum-Mullum's initial instructions:

*Think not you can return on the path that leads to the
fork.*
Taken once, it disappears as the choice lies ahead.

She took a deep breath and walked forward.

In the Outer Circle:

Once inside, Vera felt perfectly fine. She was on a line
with many other people. It looked like a circus. It was a mild
afternoon, and the air hung with an unhurried expectancy.
Lan-Lan was beside her. She liked standing next to him
because he had a commanding presence, and people looked
at him as if he were a celebrity or royalty.

When seated and waiting for the show to begin, Vera
noticed something peculiar about the circus staff. There
seemed to be two distinct uniforms: one brown and one soft
blue. The brown-uniformed staff were at the entrance scanning the tickets, while the blue-uniformed staff, who seemed
to have a slight glow around them, were walking up and
down the aisles rescanning people's tickets.

"Why are they rescanning the tickets?" Vera asked Lan-
Lan. "They already did it at the entrance."

"They are looking for something," said Lan-Lan. "The
brown ones are referred to as the ticket scammers and the
blue ones as the ticket scanners. But that's an inside joke."

Vera did not feel that she was on the inside of that joke.

"The brown ones don't know they are scammers," said
Lan-Lan. "They are trained to uphold an order that is delusional. The blue ones are there to disillusion."

There were several peculiar things about the blue ticket

scanners. They weren't checking everyone's tickets—it seemed rather random. Most people did not appear to see them and would try to walk straight through them. The scanners would merge into the crowd and reform nearby. Vera noticed that they were scanning tickets not with a machine, but with their thumbs.

One of them appeared by her side. By now, Vera was a little unnerved by them. Lan-Lan smiled at her and indicated to hold out her ticket. As the ticket scanner ran his thumb over the barcode, the lines rearranged themselves into a different order. Vera stared at her ticket and then at the ticket scanner. The ticket scanner stared at Vera, then Lan-Lan, and promptly left.

CHAPTER 16
REMEMBER

In the Outer Circle:

The blue ticket scanners were not the only thing most people seemed unaware of. Of graver concern was a prominent, black figure with a cloak. It was about ten feet tall and wore a hood that covered most of its face. It had a malevolent energy field. Although the ticket scanners knew it was there, they, for the most part, ignored it. It, however, was watching them closely to see their scanning results.

"Who is that?" asked Vera, pointing to the creature.

"It is the Dream Maker," said Lan-Lan.

"That sounds innocent enough," said Vera, unconvinced.

"It is far from innocuous," said Lan-Lan. "Its dreams are highly deceptive and vicious."

After the ticket scanner departed, the dark creature headed Vera's way. It was looming over her. She could see the eyes of the creature. They were red and fiery but also cold and blank.

"What does it want?" Vera said to Lan-Lan as she grabbed his arm.

"It wants your memory," said Lan-Lan.

"Make it go away," said Vera.

"I can't," said Lan-Lan. "It is here by consent of every person who ever came here."

Vera tentatively turned to the creature. Although it was peering at her, demanding something, it didn't seem to be able to take it without her permission.

"I remember who you are," said Vera turning to Lan-Lan in a strike of revelation. "You are Lan-Lan, Lord of Long Hill, and I am Vera, Lady Faith of the Inner Circle."

The dark creature withdrew, bitterness draping from its shoulders. The blue ticket scanners formed a circle around Vera and Lan-Lan and merged into one light band. The circus noise dimmed, and Vera and Lan-Lan stood in the now quiet room.

"The Outer Circle is made of dreams," said Lan-Lan, "which are fed by the Dream Maker. If one remembers that one is here for something more than fragile dreams, one will have passed the first pivotal test."

Vera recollected that Mullum-Mullum told her, "The most common reaction of those who get to the first circle, the Outer Circle, is to abandon the quest immediately."

"I see," said Vera. "The quest is not abandoned deliberately and consciously. It is abandoned because we cannot remember what we are doing. The mission is aborted before it is even started."

"Congratulations," said Lan-Lan. "You may now proceed beyond the Outer Circle."

CHAPTER 17
FAULT

ON EARTH

Back in Waldmeer:

Amira tried to keep baby Lan-Lan away from Gabriel. It wasn't always possible. She had to have him when Ide was at work, and Ide's shifts at the hospital varied. Gabriel didn't want children. He certainly didn't want someone else's children, least of all Farkas's. Lately, Lan-Lan had been there a lot when Gabriel was home.

This morning, Gabriel was complaining about everything, stomping around, and generally being painful.

"I know whose child it is," he blurted out accusingly. "I'm not that dumb."

"Really?" said Amira.

Gabriel scowled at her.

"I mean, really, you know whose child it is. I didn't mean, really, you're not that dumb."

She was making it worse.

Gabriel had never asked her which friend she was

helping out, so she had never told him. She knew it wasn't a great solution, but she couldn't think of another. She sighed. It was Gabriel's home, too, and his life. He had a right to live as he wished. The problem was that she couldn't not have Lan-Lan.

"I don't understand why he can't look after his own frickin' kid, himself," said Gabriel. "And now I feel bad because Lan-Lan is just a baby, and it's not his fault."

Lan-Lan was playing happily on the floor. Little children are terribly resilient. Gabriel grabbed his work things and stormed out the door.

"Oh dear," said Amira to Lan-Lan. "What will we do?"

Lan-Lan prattled on with some helpful baby advice. If only they both knew what he was saying.

IMPERFECT

CHAPTER 18
UNDYING

Thomas and Kathleen sat in their favourite city restaurant, the Afghan Light. They were enthusiastically discussing Thomas's new retirement plan. Kathleen was very pleased with his decision and felt it would do him a world of good. Thomas had mixed emotions —excitement, terror, serenity, emptiness. Every time he veered towards one of the more unproductive feelings, Kathleen reminded him that he had achieved so much at school, but now it was time for something new and wonderful.

"I know you are right," said Thomas, "but then I start wondering if it's all a big mistake."

"Well then, you don't really know that I am right," said Kathleen. "You only half know."

Thomas laughed.

The restaurant owner approached their table. His name was Herat. He had moved from Afghanistan twenty-five years ago but was still proudly steeped in his heritage.

When Thomas and Kathleen first started coming to the Afghan Light, Herat always shook Thomas's hand but never

Kathleen's. He would nod to her, put his hand on his chest, and say Assalamu Alaykum (peace be unto you). One day, Kathleen asked Herat's wife if her husband didn't like to shake hands with women.

"He would not touch you uninvited," said Herat's wife. "If you hold out your hand, he will gladly take it."

On their next visit to the restaurant, Kathleen hesitantly held out her hand to Herat. Herat rushed to take her hand and warmly shook it. From then on, Kathleen decided she rather liked the hand-on-heart gesture that he previously did and never bothered him again to shake hands.

This evening, Herat said to Thomas, "My friend, I have something for you. It is to commemorate the beginning of a new stage of life for you. Follow me, please."

Thomas and Kathleen looked at each other with keen interest and followed Herat into the back of the shop. The restaurant was small. Thomas and Kathleen assumed that the back area was for staff only.

Herat led them to a darkish staircase and beckoned them down. Once their eyes were accustomed to the low light, they could see that the stairway was lined with antique rugs. It led to a corridor that was also carpet-lined. The passage led to a windowless back room piled high with hundreds of exquisite, handmade Afghan rugs. Something about the room was magical. Thomas and Kathleen were enthralled, and Herat's eyes lit up.

In the middle of the room was an antique coffee table. On the table was a blue porcelain teapot with a hand-painted floral motif. Herat poured green tea from it and passed them silver trays of pistachios, raisins, almonds, and traditional sweets.

"Please," said Herat, "sit and eat. We will wait for the decision."

Thomas and Kathleen wondered what the decision was deciding and for whom, but they didn't want to break the sacred atmosphere by asking. They sat, ate, and waited. Herat paced the room.

After ten minutes, he eagerly announced, "It is this one. They have decided."

He pointed to one of the rugs with a corner poking out from the enormous pile.

"It did have to be one at the bottom of the pile," joked Herat as he pulled the top rugs off to get to the chosen one.

Thomas jumped to his feet to help his friend. They grabbed an end of each rug and made a new pile while Herat told little stories about the carpets. He remembered where each one came from and how it had served its previous owners.

"We value these rugs more for the service they have already given," said Herat.

Having reached the chosen rug, Herat pulled it out ceremoniously.

"It's magnificent," said Kathleen.

It was a vibrant, intense red with a traditional, hand-knotted elephant foot design.

"It has two faults—one from wear and tear and an intentional fault," said Herat. "The intentional fault is woven into the rug because only God is perfect. I will not tell you where it is. That is for you to discover."

Thomas ran his hand over the thick rug. His hand came to a small hole in one corner.

"Is this it?" asked Thomas.

"No," said Herat. "That is the wear and tear fault. This

rug was owned by a family whose child was very sick for months. The family dog refused to leave the child and eventually made a hole in the rug where it lay. Praise Allah, the child recovered. Undying love and healing are in this rug."

Herat looked at Thomas with eyes as deep as the rug's rich darkness and said, "That is why it belongs to you. Use it well. They have given you a fine gift."

CHAPTER 19
FAITH

INTER-DIMENSIONAL

n the inter-dimensional Long Hill:

"Would you like to know what baby Lan-Lan was saying?" said Lord Lan-Lan to Vera. "Babies do not have both feet on Earth. They float between worlds and cannot clearly distinguish them. As they grow, they become established as Earth dwellers, and the memory of other worlds fades. Baby Lan-Lan was trying to convey his higher wisdom."

Lord Lan-Lan and Vera were sitting inside his home in Long Hill. Vera was surprised to be back in Long Hill. She found herself amongst its familiar green hills, outside a sweet weatherboard cottage with an old slate roof. She didn't expect Lan-Lan's house to look like this.

"Were you expecting a castle?" Lan-Lan asked with a smile. "When you have a castle within, you don't need one outside. I prefer to keep things simple."

It was a lovely, clean, and thoughtfully decorated home.

Lan-Lan explained that, as Vera had remembered her spiritual name of Lady Faith, she was entitled to come and go to Long Hill whenever she wished.

Standing up and walking to the window, he surveyed the garden, a delightful mixture of delicate flowers and magnificent trees. He watched two residents of Long Hill, a man and a woman, sit under an oak tree.

Changing the topic, he said, "The lords and ladies of Long Hill do not have sexual relationships or even exclusive personal relationships. They do not need physical gratification. It is child's play to them. They also have no need for emotional pairing with other beings. Every lord and lady feels intimately joined with all other beings."

"If I lived like that on Earth," said Vera, "it wouldn't work."

"You have a purpose there," said Lan-Lan. "You must live as a human—knowing the body, the human struggle, and recalling the way out. On Earth, relationships are necessary. They are how people learn to love, and are the medium best suited to Earth people."

"It is one thing for *me* to know this," said Vera, "and quite another for others to."

"Love unites," said Lan-Lan. "It speaks its own language, and that language is always unifying."

"One more thing," said Lan-Lan as Vera was leaving, "Be patient. It may get worse before it gets better."

CHAPTER 20
DRESSED-UP DELUSION

ON EARTH

Back in Waldmeer:
Gabriel didn't come home after work on the day he got upset about baby Lan-Lan. He messaged Amira that he was staying in Darnall, the town of the college, for a party. He had a group of gay friends in Darnall. They were generally referred to as the Boys of Darnall, although they were all men and a few select women. Some of them were associated with the college, and that is how Gabriel came to develop the friendship with them.

He messaged the following night to say that he was going to stay in Darnall for the week as someone was away, and he could use their house. It was right next to the college.

TEXT MESSAGE FROM AMIRA

> What about your clothes?

GABRIEL

It's fine. I can borrow some of theirs. They won't care.

No, they won't care, thought Amira. *They will like it!* The Boys of Darnall were always trying to win Gabriel back into the flock.

Amira missed him already, but some things are more important than missing—like love. People have to come back if and when they are ready. Then, they will come back in the right way or, at the very least, with the right bargains. Every other arrangement can only be a dressed-up delusion.

BRICK WALL

CHAPTER 21
THE HATTERY

A few years ago, when Amira first returned to Waldmeer from Eraldus, she had an unfortunate experience with a Waldmeer couple, Oswald and Billy. They were domestic and business partners and owned the upmarket Hattery on the main street of Waldmeer. A narrow path between the brick walls of two buildings led to a plain, black door which was the entrance to the exclusive shop. It didn't even have a sign.

"We want our reputation to speak for itself," said Oswald. "The people will find us."

"The right people," added Billy with a touch of snobbery.

The Hattery sold men's hats. Both the shop and the owners were chic and edgy. Oswald and Billy designed and often made the hats themselves. The Hattery had an assortment of boutique hats—Ecuadorian panamas, Fred Astaire fedoras, aristocratic bowlers, summer boaters, casual and cool newsboys, versatile and stylish beanies, and glamorous top hats.

"We sell everything but baseball caps," said Billy.

"We don't do cheap and nasty," said Oswald. "We aren't in the business of covering middle-aged, balding heads. We do fashion."

Although Oswald and Billy advertised their hattery as a place for the modern gentleman, they were often heard to say to their adoring female fan base, "If men's hats were good enough for Marlene Dietrich, they are good enough for you, darling."

The store was tastefully crammed with fine hats, but it also had a corner dedicated to other items—books, cards, and ornaments. Everything in that corner had something of a spiritual element. And that is how Amira originally became interested in the men and their shop. Anyway, technically, Oswald and Billy were the new folk, and she was the local. She wanted to be welcoming.

Billy looked like a well-dressed gentleman from the 1940s, even though he was only around thirty-five. Slim, fine-featured, impeccably groomed, and equally impeccably mannered. He was the first to smile and engage with the customers and was unfailingly polite and attentive.

Oswald was different. About five years older, he had more fire inside him. He had a passion for life and a simmering pain that seemed to burst out periodically. He would then rely on Billy to fix everything up.

The men had been together for about seven years. Billy adored Oswald. Without Oswald, Billy was boring. Oswald needed Billy. Without Billy, Oswald got lost.

They tended to make a big to-do about their relationship and were used to a responsive crowd, *Oh, aren't they cute? Don't they love each other? The perfect couple.* Amira thought that sort of thing was silly about straight couples and equally silly about gay ones.

CHAPTER 22
STONEWALLING

Amira called into the Hattery frequently in the early days to say hello and browse. She soon started talking about her healing work. Her practice was new in Waldmeer, and, in retrospect, she was probably a little too keen to share it at that stage. The wisdom of perspective usually comes *after* the event.

Oswald was genuinely interested. He was particularly impressed by anything psychic or unusual. Novice seekers look for validation of their newfound leanings. As Oswald became more interested in Amira and her work, Billy became more suspicious. Amira realised that Billy's gentlemanly smile was only given if one did not threaten to disturb his life.

Whenever she called into the shop, Oswald would eagerly take up their conversation from where they left off last time, but Billy's jealousy and dislike were intensifying.

Billy thinks if Oswald changes, then their relationship will be at risk, thought Amira. *Maybe, he is right.*

Although Amira understood Billy's fear and did not want to cause him stress, it was more important to her that a soul grow. Life would have to take its course. It did.

One morning, Amira walked into the shop and was greeted by icy silence. Oswald remained at the back of the shop, and Billy came to meet her.

"Good morning, Amira," said Billy. "May I help you?"

May I help you? thought Amira. *I always come in here, and Oswald always talks to me. I don't want your help, Billy, because you don't like me.*

"Ah, no," said Amira. "Thank you. I'm just browsing."

She picked up a hat as if considering it, although it would have looked absurd on her. She put it down awkwardly and left. She found it difficult to accept that her budding friendship with Oswald had abruptly aborted. She tried, on numerous occasions, to call into the shop or wave to Oswald and Billy in the street. Each time, they reciprocated with a brick wall.

She was hurt, not so much by Billy but by Oswald. She knew that Billy thought he was fighting for his relationship. Fear can turn a manicured gentleness into a snarling critter. However, she felt she had developed a genuine connection with Oswald. He had abandoned ship, and left her on the sinking one with not a backward glance.

Occasionally, if Amira saw Oswald when Billy wasn't with him, she would see a different look on his face. Probably, it was guilt. However, if Amira gave him even the slightest positive response, he would walk off as if she were pursuing him with unwanted advances.

Is his concept of love so limited? wondered Amira. *Any relationship that intentionally harms others for the "sake" of the relationship is on a very shaky foundation.*

That was more than two years ago, and Oswald and Billy were still going strong.

CHAPTER 23
LONELY

G abriel had been in Darnall for the last week and a half. Amira messaged him to suggest she drop off some of his clothes the next time she was heading Darnall way. He would surely need his things by now.

GABRIEL

Thanks. The owners of the house I've been staying in are coming back from their holiday today. They have a shop in Waldmeer, the Hattery, down the path between the big brick walls to the black door.

AMIRA

Yes, I know it. I believe the owners are Oswald and Billy. Is that whose house you are staying in?

Amira had never mentioned Oswald or Billy to Gabriel. At the time of her problem with them, Gabriel was busy in

Eraldus, and Amira didn't see him much. When she did, she didn't want to bother him with her troubles. Even though she had never mentioned them to him, she was fairly sure they would soon mention her to him in a less than complimentary manner.

GABRIEL

Can you please take a bag of my clothes to the shop and they will bring it back to Darnall after work tomorrow.

AMIRA

Sure.

IT WAS Gabriel's 40th birthday the following week. The Boys of Darnall decided to throw him a party at the one and only nightclub in Darnall. Even though the nightclub couldn't compete with a fashionable city nightclub, the Boys did their best to keep it as on-point as possible. Although it didn't seem a particularly good idea, Gabriel messaged Amira to invite her as he couldn't not invite her to his 40th.

Amira had never been to a nightclub. She was, and always had been, more interested in convents than clubs. The drinking, noise, darkness, packed bodies, meaningless conversations, uncensored sexuality, and blatant craving for human connection were the antithesis of who she was. She felt it was the antithesis of who anyone really was.

Having no idea what to wear, she asked her two girlfriends, Teresa and Ide. Teresa was no help. She was too... bohemian. Ide wasn't a help either. She was too..., er, Irish.

Amira decided to go to the young, trendy clothes shop in Waldmeer. The sales assistant was, indeed, young. She was only eighteen. She was very willing to help, but everything she gave Amira to try on was too short, clingy, see-through, or generally ridiculous. Amira ended up buying the only dress that was passable. Just.

The following Saturday was the party. From the moment Gabriel saw Amira, he looked worried. He could have been embarrassed by her obvious lack of fitting in, but it wasn't that. He knew that the Boys of Darnall could be mean and that she would make little effort to oblige with small talk. He felt that she would probably end up standing there, not bothering to correct the awkwardness of the situation.

He tried several times to take her with him and introduce her to a few people, but nothing worked. He couldn't stay with her because everyone in the room wanted to talk to him. Amira would have left, but she felt it would be too obvious. In the end, Oswald approached her. He would likely say something nasty, she assumed.

"You don't belong here," said Oswald.

Amira looked at him. His eyes were softer than usual. She wasn't sure if he was humiliating or saving her. He pointed to the back door, a few steps behind them. He seemed to be suggesting that she could slip out without anyone noticing, which is exactly what she did.

AFTER A FORTY-FIVE-MINUTE DRIVE on the dark country road, she arrived home. Far from feeling lonely, the winding, empty road and reassuring night sky helped to restore her sanity and equilibrium.

Nothing could be lonelier than that club, thought Amira.

Once home, she turned on the lights and heating, took off her dress, put it in the bin, and said aloud, "If Gabriel wants to be part of my life, we will have to meet on neutral ground. I will not ask him to be more than he can or wants to be, but I will not be less than I am."

CHAPTER 24
TREASURE

INTER-DIMENSIONAL

In the middle of the night, Amira woke up. She didn't wake up as Vera. Nor was she in Long Hill or one of the Circles. She woke up as Amira, in Waldmeer.

That's strange, she thought. *Why am I here?*

She opened a black door.

The Hattery, she thought.

As she entered, she noticed moving boxes in one of the corners. Billy approached her. He had a warm and trusting smile.

"Hi," said Billy shaking her hand, "My name is Billy. Sorry, we still haven't finished unpacking but welcome to the Hattery. Please look around."

"Thanks," said Amira.

It must be when the shop first opened, thought Amira.

She glanced towards one of the many shop mirrors.

Yes, I do have a few less lines, she thought approvingly.

She walked to the corner with the spiritual knickknacks.

Oswald approached her and said, "They are nice, aren't they? Do you have an interest in things like that?"

"Yes," said Amira carefully.

"Oh, I love stuff like that," said Oswald passionately. "We must talk."

He took her arm and looked like he had just discovered an exciting treasure.

"One day," said Amira, "when you are ready."

Oswald thought she meant that he would be too busy setting up shop right now.

"I'm never too busy for a real conversation," he protested.

Amira released her arm from Oswald's hand, smiled back at him with forgiving but distant eyes, and left.

ADJUSTMENTS

CHAPTER 25
VIBES

ON EARTH

In Waldmeer:

The rain was bucketing down, and the wind was gusting fiercely and unpredictably. Never one to give up on her walks, Amira set off down the hill to town. After a few minutes, she abandoned her umbrella, pulled her hood over her head, and sped up her pace. By the time she got to the yoga studio, she was as wet as the day.

"You're a sight for sore eyes after almost two years," said Sri.

He laughed and handed her a towel.

"I'll hug you when you are dry," he said.

Sri wasn't his birth name. Amira didn't know his birth name, but his full Sanskrit name was Sri Farook Roshan. Sri is a term of respect. Farook means *moral*. Roshan means *shining light*. As Waldmeerians didn't understand that Sri was a title of esteem within the yoga community, they assumed it was his first name and started calling him that. Besides, it was the easiest of the three names to remember.

The studio, Vibes, was set up by Sri and his partner, Gloria, around the same time the Hattery opened. It was Waldmeer's introduction to yoga.

In the same way that Amira had welcomed Oswald and Billy, she embraced Sri and Gloria, all the more because they were exponents of the spiritual path. Although Amira was delighted to have them in town, the townsfolk, on the whole, were suspicious of them with their Vedic philosophy, Sanskrit chanting, motivational banners, and loud whale-calling music.

Early on, Amira received this warm letter from Gloria.

My partner and I are thrilled to receive your welcome note. Sri and I came together through yoga ten years ago and have grown ever since as a couple and as professional yoga teachers. We both fell in love with Waldmeer when we were here on holiday and dreamed that, one day, we would bring yoga to Waldmeer. Finally, our dream has come true. It's lovely to know that you are here doing your healing work. We are on the same wavelength. We would love to have you in our classes. It will be nice to have someone who doesn't think we are a cult!

Love and light, Gloria

Sri was charming, confident, and outgoing. He soon won over many of the town's residents. He would go to all the hangouts of the middle-aged Waldmeer women—the cafes, parks, church halls, bowling and golf clubs—and wooed his way into their hearts as he hugged and complimented them.

He was middle-aged himself, but after thirty years of yoga, he was a picture of health. His vibrant, young attitude took years off him. The attendance at his classes rapidly grew. Once won over, the wives and mothers of Waldmeer were a force to be reckoned with. They protected Sri from the naysayers. In return, he loved them and changed their bodies and outlook.

Gloria also taught classes. She was the backbone of the studio in terms of its day-to-day functioning. Her knowledge of yoga was just as good as Sri's, and after a while, the students started to appreciate her teaching in its own right, even if it didn't have the flair of her more charismatic partner. Sri's most loyal devotee was Gloria.

Sometimes, Amira wondered why Sri was with Gloria. He could have done *better*. He had many opportunities. Amira felt he probably took up some of those opportunities, but he would have been careful. It would have been women who were ethical enough not to hurt Gloria but not ethical enough to say no to him.

Occasionally, Sri would say that he and Gloria were like brother and sister. He would say it even when Gloria was in the room. It was meant to sound like a compliment, but a partner is not a sibling. Gloria would tense up when he said it. Like everything else he did that bothered her, she smiled and said, "We are blessed."

Something was keeping them together. Once, Amira overheard a private conversation between Gloria and Sri.

"You must stop being so hard on yourself," Sri said. "All day long, you say such mean things to yourself. Why do you do that? There is no need. You are beautiful."

Amira looked at Gloria, and for a moment, she truly looked beautiful. The insecurity was gone and replaced with a content, intelligent calmness.

Although Amira wanted it to work at the studio, she didn't end up staying long. After Gloria's first letter, Amira never felt the same warmth from her again. Instead of making a friend of Amira or, at least, a spiritual and professional peer, Gloria tried to assert her superiority over Amira.

She would help and adjust every other class member, but never Amira. She would ask all the members to demonstrate asanas, but never Amira. She would ask her students' thoughts but "accidentally" skip Amira as she went around the circle.

Amira persevered in the hope of helping Gloria realise that they were on the same team. The day that she saw outright hatred on Gloria's face was the day she left her classes.

Amira had also been attending Sri's classes, probably exacerbating her problem with Gloria. Sri liked Amira immediately and didn't hide it. Sri liked most people, especially women. They tended to be his willing fans. Amira did not think like that. She doubted it would even be possible for her to view another person like that, let alone someone who used his sexuality to build a fan base. She liked Sri. There was much to like, and he was a fellow student of the path. But even if he was single, she would not be interested in him personally. He was a player. Amira didn't play. And, if she did, it was for keeps.

Although Gloria never adjusted Amira in her classes, Sri adjusted her every opportunity he got. He was very hands-on in his adjustments. One particular day, he held Amira so close that she could feel not only both his hips but what was between his hips as well. As it was in front of the whole class, she was taken aback but felt she couldn't do much about it. Sri felt her body tense, and he moved away. He never forced his way onto women. He seduced them. That was the last time Amira went to Sri's classes.

It was now two years on, and Amira thought that she would give Vibes another try. As Gabriel was away, maybe permanently away for all she knew, she was trying to do a few new things so that she would not be thinking about him too much. Apparently, Sri and Gloria had had a baby who would be about the same age as Lan-Lan. Babies change people. Life changes people. It was time to try again.

CHAPTER 26
LOVE AND LIGHT

Amira often took Lan-Lan to the park in the morning. It was on the grass reserve between the sea and the shops. Lan-Lan would have a swing and play in the sandpit. He was easy to look after as he wasn't old enough to go far by his own steam. Amira would look out over the blue expanse of sea. It was an enjoyable outing for both.

This morning, there was a similar-aged child already in the baby swing.

"Never mind, Lan-Lan," said Amira. "We will wait."

Lan-Lan smiled in his usual, complacent manner. She kissed his chubby cheek. It was so squishy, and he was so kissable.

"Now, that's a loved-up child," said the Dad at the swing as he turned around.

It was Sri.

"Is there something I don't know about?" asked Sri as he pointed to Lan-Lan.

"No," laughed Amira. "He's my friend's baby."

Sri picked up his baby and said to Lan-Lan, "Here you go, young man. The swing is free. We have to go."

He waved goodbye and said loud enough for anyone nearby to hear, "Remember to spread the peace-vibes. We are the love and light of the world."

When Sri was out of earshot, another voice said, "He's a bit of a wanker, isn't he?"

Lan-Lan reached in the direction of the voice. It was Farkas. Father and son were very happy to see each other again. Amira didn't want to interrupt their special reuniting. She waited until Farkas was free to talk. Lan-Lan was preoccupied with a stick on the ground.

"Who was that?" asked Farkas. "I'm hoping not your new boyfriend."

"No," smiled Amira. "He and his partner own the yoga studio."

"So how is your old boyfriend then?" asked Farkas.

"Gabriel is fine," said Amira, "I think. I'm not sure because he's been staying in Darnall."

"With the Boys of Darnall?" asked Farkas. "Has he changed his mind... again?"

"I don't know," said Amira.

"Is he *with* any of them?" asked Farkas.

"I don't think so," said Amira. "If he thinks we are still together, he wouldn't be."

Farkas nodded.

"Anyway, I don't think it's about *that*," continued Amira. "Is sex that important to base a whole major life decision on?"

"Of course it is," said Farkas.

"For someone who gets lots of offers that don't get taken up," said Amira, "you seem pretty sure about that."

Farkas smiled and then said more seriously, "I think he's scared."

"Of what?" asked Amira.

"A relationship where he has to tell the truth," said Farkas.

He bent down to pick up a piece of rubbish that Lan-Lan had uncovered in the sand pit and said, "I'll take that, my boy."

Turning back to Amira, he continued, "Maybe it's because you ask too much."

"Too much of what?" asked Amira.

"I don't know what it is," said Farkas, "but it's too much."

"What I ask is for the good of the other person," said Amira.

"In your mind, it is," said Farkas, "but not necessarily in the other person's."

Amira watched the white cockatoos surround an unsuspecting tourist who had hot chips. They were getting closer and closer. The visitor panicked, threw his chips in the air, and ran away. A mass of squawking birds dived, and then it was all over.

"Oh dear, they're such bullies," said Amira. "I went to Gabriel's 40th in the Darnall nightclub last week."

Farkas laughed and said, "I can imagine how well that went. Why did you go?"

"Yes, it was a disaster," said Amira. "I suppose, in retrospect, it's funny, but I can assure you that it wasn't funny at the time."

Somehow, the memory of it seemed a little lighter for

someone else laughing at it. The whole time Amira had been talking with Farkas, he had been playing with Lan-Lan.

"This is the first morning I've been out of the Leleks," said Farkas. "I'm working on Erdo's farm, and he asked me to come into Waldmeer to do some errands."

"I didn't know Erdo had a farm," said Amira.

How peculiar that Erdo never mentioned it, thought Amira.

"I have to go now," said Farkas handing Lan-Lan to Amira.

"Ide misses you," said Amira.

"I didn't sleep with Elise even though Ide probably thinks I did," said Farkas.

"I know you didn't," said Amira.

"Tell Ide," said Farkas, "that I think about her and Lan-Lan every day."

Amira nodded and said goodbye cheerfully so as not to upset Lan-Lan with sad goodbyes.

At that moment, a lady crossed the road from the shops and called out to Farkas repeatedly.

"Farkas, it's me."

She waved at him madly.

"It's the lady from the Opportunity Shop," whispered Farkas.

"Hello, Amelia," said Farkas. "How are you?"

"You remember my name," said Amelia.

"Of course," said Farkas. "Amelia, this is my friend, Amira, and my son, Lan-Lan."

Amelia ignored Amira and pinched Lan-Lan's cheek.

"Oh, you are as handsome as your father," said Amelia.

Turning to Farkas, she said, "The ladies and I would love you to join our tennis group. Can you come next week?"

Amira couldn't help smiling and looked at Farkas as if to say, *Well?*

"I'm very busy with work at the moment," said Farkas. "In fact, I'm already late. Bye, ladies."

Amelia didn't bother to say goodbye to Amira. She just walked off.

"Come on, Lan-Lan," said Amira. "It's a beautiful day. We have every reason to be happy."

CHAPTER 27
RIGHT OR WRONG

That afternoon, when Ide picked up Lan-Lan, she got a message.

"It's Farkas," she said to Amira.

> **FARKAS**
>
> I'm thinking of coming home for the weekend and then returning to work for the week. Okay?

Ide stared at the message and then at Amira. Lan-Lan was leaping out of Amira's arms to get to his mother.

"Daddy's back," Ide said to Lan-Lan.

THE FOLLOWING MORNING, Amira was weeding the garden. It was an exquisite morning. Everything was bewitching—the sky, the sea at the bottom of the hill, the forest behind her, the garden with its joyous, little microcosm of activity and togetherness. It was all casting a spell.

What a glad and fortunate spell it is, thought Amira. *If we could live in the consecrated space of happiness and forget the past, how easily the world would transform.*

When she returned to the house, she noticed a missed call from Gabriel.

"Did you ring me?" she asked when she called back.

"Um, did I ring?" said Gabriel distractedly.

"Yes, did you ring me?" repeated Amira.

"Oh, yes. Yes, I did," said Gabriel, gathering his thoughts. "Can you do me a favour?"

Amira didn't say anything and waited for Gabriel to continue.

"The psychology department at the College is running a program with the Dementia Unit of the local hospital."

"Yes," said Amira, wondering what this would have to do with her.

"One of the activities is a ballroom dancing class. They feel that the dancing and music from the patients' era will help to stimulate their memory."

"We only did one year of dance classes in Eraldus," said Amira, seeing where this was going.

"They're desperate," said Gabriel. "The person they had lined up can't do it. It's just for tonight. Then they'll be able to find someone more qualified."

Amira hesitated but said, "Okay. Why not? It'll be fun. Anyway, they won't be able to remember if we're right or wrong."

"See you tonight," said Gabriel. "7.30 at the hospital. Gotta run. Bye."

"Bye," said Amira, but Gabriel was already gone.

CHOOSE AGAIN

CHAPTER 28
DRAMA

Amira took every opportunity to be outside on that crisp, glorious day. She walked down to the beach and returned via the shops and up the hill, taking the longer route past Verloren's holiday house. There was a *For Sale* sign in the front garden. She stopped to look at it and wondered why Verloren would be selling.

In the five years since Farkas sold this house to Verloren, thought Amira, *he has lived at Charlie's property in the back hills and in Ide's bungalow, bought a house, started a relationship, had a baby, ended a relationship, and is now, hopefully, resurrecting that same relationship.*

What Amira didn't recall was Farkas's two inter-dimensional trips to the North Country—one to the wolf pack for a whole winter and one to the Head Gardener's house in the Garden of Garourinn.

Verloren had also been given the privilege of an inter-dimensional visit to the Garden of Garourinn in her earliest Waldmeer days. Its value seemed to lie dormant for the many years since. Verloren did occasionally dream of the

Head Gardener. She didn't know who he was other than a wise man giving advice. Generally, she couldn't recall what the advice had been.

"Hello," said Verloren as she came from the side walkway and saw Amira standing in front of her sign. "As you see, we are selling. I am sick of the small-minded mentality in this town."

"Oh, that's a pity," said Amira.

She wanted Verloren to grow, not go.

"Is it a pity?" said Verloren. "For years, I have tried to get these people," she waved down the hill as if waving at the peasants below, "to accept and appreciate me. They can't see anything except their own petty lives."

Now that Verloren had virtually no contact with Farkas, her previous attitude to Amira had improved. Now and again, Amira thought that she even saw a tiny, budding desire for friendship. A different friendship to what Verloren was accustomed to—not to boost her ego, support her gripes and dramas, or further any cause she had in mind, but friendship for its own sake.

Changing her tone, Verloren said, "Since I have put my house up for sale, I have had several dreams that a man keeps telling me, 'Don't change your location. Change your approach.'"

"Really?" said Amira. "That's interesting. In what way?"

"He says something like, 'Don't feed the drama monster. It's insatiable and has no friends.' I don't understand it," said Verloren, "because I don't look for drama. It looks for me!"

"Hmm," said Amira. "It's a spectacular afternoon, so maybe just enjoy it."

Verloren looked at the sky with its vast, endless blue and said, "It is spectacular, isn't it?"

"I have to go now," said Amira. "I'm going into Darnall this evening to help Gabriel with a group of dementia patients."

"That's nice of you," said Verloren.

"I don't know how nice it is," smiled Amira. "We are supposed to teach them dancing, and neither of us knows what we are doing. It may not be nice at all."

CHAPTER 29
NOT WELL OR SICK

That evening, Thomas sat in his lounge room admiring the majestic rug Herat had recently given him. He wondered where the intentional fault that Herat had spoken of was and why he had given him a gift with "undying love and healing" in it. Amidst his wonderings, his phone rang. It was Kathleen.

That's strange, thought Thomas. *Kathleen rarely rings me. She waits for me to ring her because she doesn't know my schedule.*

"How are you?" asked Thomas with concern.

"Hi," said Kathleen. "I'm fine, but there's a little issue."

"Yes?" said Thomas.

If it were "little", she wouldn't concern me with it at all, he thought.

"You know that I don't take much notice of medical opinions," said Kathleen. "I suppose that's peculiar because I was involved with the medical field for so long."

Kathleen's deceased husband was a doctor.

"The people with the worst health seem to be the ones

most concerned about their health," she said. "And those with the best health seem to be the least concerned about their health."

"Maybe, the well ones are not concerned with their health because they are well," said Thomas half-heartedly.

His mind was racing with scenarios about Kathleen.

"Perhaps," said Kathleen, "but I feel it's the other way around. Anyway, to not cause a fuss, I do all those annoying tests that women over fifty are supposed to do."

Kathleen's voice faltered.

"You are the only person I am telling this to. I have received a troubling test result today, and I need to see a specialist in the next few weeks."

Thomas was still. When something really mattered, Thomas became a different person. Not completely different, but a higher version of himself. It had happened to him numerous times in his life, but he didn't understand what he was doing. It was the healing gift.

"I see," said Thomas after a lengthy pause. "You are not to worry about this because you will be well and happy. Nothing is going to hurt you. Further, I think it may be a fortuitous opportunity for us to go on a holiday for a few weeks.

"What about work?" asked Kathleen.

"My deputy can take over. I have years of leave accrued. So, where would you like to go? On a cruise?"

"No," said Kathleen emphatically. "I can't think of anything worse than being stuck in a confined space with indulgent people, indulging in massive amounts of food and indulgent, endless entertainment. No."

"Okay," laughed Thomas.

He loved cruises.

"It's not a busy time of year for tourists," said Thomas. "It's cold. Why don't we set out in the car and decide what to do as we travel? We are old enough to trust that life will show us where to go and how to get there."

"Agreed," said Kathleen. "There is one other person that I have told."

"Who?" asked Thomas.

"My brother, Aishi," said Kathleen.

Aishi was a monk who worked in a retreat centre in the hills outside the city.

"Oh, yes," said Thomas. "Of course. What did he say?"

"He said, 'When the body is in its rightful mode, it is silent. We feel neither well nor sick, healthy nor unhealthy. The body becomes the quiet, perfectly functioning tool by which God uses us in this life. Your body can be well just as easily as sick. Your life can be harmonious and glad as easily as tormented and dramatic. Choose carefully. And if you have chosen unfortunately, then choose again.'"

"I will pick you up after work this Friday," said Thomas.

CHAPTER 30
DON'T TELL ME

I*n Darnall:*

"You look so much younger without any facial hair," said Teresa to Bryan that evening in one of the Darnall restaurants.

They had driven there separately as it was easier for Bryan to go straight to Darnall from the farm rather than drive via Waldmeer. He had dressed up and shaved. It was their first outing since breaking up. Teresa looked at Bryan's fresh, young face and the ten-year age gap seemed more obvious than ever before.

"You are not allowed to say that I look so much older when I do certain things," laughed Teresa.

Bryan laughed too but decided it was best not to say anything, even in jest, in their current circumstances.

After the meal, Bryan said, "I want to be upfront with you."

"Aren't we always?" said Teresa.

Bryan frowned a bit and looked at Teresa as if to say, *You were not upfront with me about not wanting to get married.*

He said, "I've been on a date with one of my old school friends."

As Teresa and Bryan were both locals of Waldmeer, Teresa probably knew the woman. Her mind started checking through the women from Bryan's year level who were still single or single again. She couldn't remember who was in his year. It was too far below her. She was out of high school when he was still running around the primary school playground, getting grazed knees and plotting to steal the treasures from the girls' stick cubbies.

"If that is what you want," said Teresa, "that is what you must do."

"It's not what I want," said Bryan. "I want love, but not everyone wants that."

"Do you think you love more because you are hurt?" said Teresa. "Talk to me about love when you know what it's like to get up to someone, night after night, even though you are exhausted; when you know what it's like to take the blame for someone else's weaknesses because they can't carry it themselves; when you know what it's like to protect someone even though you will become the target of someone else's hatred; when you know what it's like to never stop praying for someone until the day that they are safe."

She stood up, put money on the table, and said, "Don't tell me what love is, Bryan."

CHAPTER 31
ELECTRICITY

The project coordinator from the Psychology Department handed Gabriel instructions and said, "This is from the dance instructor. I will be in the room with you as an observer. We want to see if the dancing program affects the patients' memories."

Gabriel read the instructions to Amira.

Tonight is Rumba.
Introduce the **side basic step**.
Weight on the left leg, side step to the right, bring the left leg in, transfer weight onto the left leg, and then transfer weight onto the right again.
Repeat on the other side.
Introduce hip action at the elementary level.
The Dementia Unit is arranging music.
Thank you for your assistance. We will be taking over, as arranged, next week.

"Let's just begin and see what happens," said Amira.

Gabriel started reading from the notes and showing the class what to do. No one moved or even listened. He put the paper on a nearby chair.

"Can anyone dance?" he asked the class.

"We can," said an elegant gentleman in his mid-eighties. "My name is Wolfgang, and this is my wife, Madeline. My wife has been in the Dementia Unit for the past year."

"Wonderful," said Gabriel.

Oops, I hope he doesn't think I'm saying wonderful to his wife having dementia, thought Gabriel.

Wolfgang continued without missing a beat, "We danced competitively decades ago and went to Blackpool many times. It was the most important international competition of the year. I presume it still is."

Some of the class members were now listening.

"Would you and Madeline like to demonstrate?" said Gabriel turning on the music.

Gabriel may not have been a dance teacher, but he was an art teacher and could read a class.

"We would love to," said Wolfgang.

He took hold of his wife's hand, and as they danced, he seemed to be regaining part of Madeline.

"We were quite a duo back then," he said. "I remember that my white jacket caused a big stir amongst all the conventional black ones. It upset the apple cart, alright. Some of the judges loved it, and some hated it. We didn't care. Who cares about judges when you have each other, and you are creating something together? Winning only matters when you don't have what dancing really is."

"I think I'd still want to win," said Gabriel.

Amira laughed. As Wolfgang and Madeline danced, Gabriel and Amira went around the class dancing with each participant. Shuffling would be more accurate, but it was enthusiastic shuffling.

"I remember," said Wolfgang to anyone who wanted to listen, "the first time I danced with Madeline. We were having a tryout. Neither of us was very good at that stage. We did the cha-cha, and it went okay. Then came rumba, the dance of love. A few steps into the dance, Madeline held her hand on my stomach. I was slightly surprised because she was a shy and proper young lady. It seemed a little forward. Not that I minded. Oh, no. You see, it was the way she touched me. I felt electricity in my body. I didn't know if other people felt it when they danced with her or only me. Either way, I wanted her."

Wolfgang smiled at Madeline, and she smiled back, although it wasn't clear if she understood anything he was saying.

"When my wife was much younger," said Wolfgang, "she would often say, 'You gotta know when to hold 'em and when to fold 'em.'"

"Did she?" asked Madeline, who suddenly found her voice but not her memory. "What a wise thing to say. I hope you held onto her."

"I did," said Wolfgang with a smile.

Later, while walking down the hallway, Amira said to Gabriel, "That was easy."

"How is Lan-Lan?" asked Gabriel.

"Cute as ever," said Amira. "It looks like Farkas may be back home, at least for the weekends. I won't have Lan-Lan quite as much."

At that moment, Wolfgang walked past and stopped to kiss Amira's hand and shake Gabriel's.

"Thank you," said Wolfgang. "You reminded me of how love makes life light up."

He walked off briskly, calling behind him, "See you next week. Before we know it, we will all be at Blackpool."

FELLOW TRAVELLERS

CHAPTER 32
UNTROUBLED

Even though Thomas and Kathleen had been boyfriend and girlfriend for two years and friends for decades, they had never been on holiday together. When Kathleen had a holiday house in Waldmeer, being in her house was her holiday. Nor had they ever lived in the same house. Their holiday was quite a revelation. It had wonderful moments and difficult ones.

Although he started in an admirable frame of mind, Thomas was very up and down over their two weeks of travelling. Sometimes, he was good. Sometimes, he was depressed, angry, in a daze, or, worst of all, needy. He had a large range of emotions.

His marriage of several decades had been based on superficial conversations. Conversations about things as important as one's chaotic emotions come from trust and a proven record that the other person can handle it. The honest mirror of a connected partner is a valuable and powerful learning opportunity.

Other than with Kathleen, Thomas had never had that

type of relationship. One gets away with a lot when one is in an unchallenging relationship or is too busy to invest in one at all. Mostly, one gets away from oneself.

Thomas's best moments were when Kathleen was afraid. He would sense it and lift himself into a better state of mind —reassuring, kind, and confident.

Thomas and Kathleen's best holiday moments together were breakfasts. They would go for an early morning walk and then choose an inviting, underpopulated cafe. They were starving after a long walk, which was perfect for breakfast. It was a luxury for Thomas to eat slowly in the morning and read the paper. They would sit quietly, reading and sharing their thoughts.

They had always been able to have interesting conversations. The mind is where they met most easily and successfully. Perhaps, it is what one would call a meeting of the minds.

Kathleen's most significant internal work was done without Thomas. She went for many long walks on her own and was not afraid to delve into the mysterious. In fact, after two weeks of soul searching, the mysterious seemed not so mysterious anymore. She felt at peace, loved, and sheltered from anything that could cause her harm.

On the last day of the holiday, when travelling in the car, Kathleen's phone beeped with a message.

"Who is that?" asked Thomas.

It was a message reminding Kathleen to confirm her upcoming appointment with the specialist. It said if she didn't confirm in the next twenty-four hours, her appointment would be given to someone else as they were in high demand.

"It's nothing," said Kathleen.

She didn't confirm the appointment.

I don't need someone to tell me if I am alright or not, thought Kathleen. *I already know.*

The sun was gentle on her face. Everything outside looked serene and in its right place. She watched the untroubled clouds passing by.

CHAPTER 33
JUST LIKE THAT

Gabriel rang to tell Amira that, apparently, Wolfgang was not happy. He didn't like the new dance instructors that they had been having for the past few weeks. He drew up a petition asking for the return of Gabriel and Amira and got all the residents of the Dementia Unit to sign it.

Understandably, the authorities thought that getting the signatures of people who would have signed anything was a questionable endeavour. Nevertheless, deciding that they had nothing to lose, Gabriel and Amira were reinstated as the dance instructors.

IN THE WALDMEER cafe that afternoon, Amira overheard a nearby conversation that caught her attention.

"Just like that," said one woman. "She returned from a trip and went to visit her daughter. Saying that she felt a little tired, she went to lie down. When the daughter returned with a glass of water, she was gone. Just like that, gone. Supposedly, she looked like she was peacefully sleeping, but, of course, the daughter was very shocked and distressed."

"All in all, it's a fantastic way to go," said the other woman. "No pain. Simply moved on."

"I heard Thomas is not taking it very well and will be taking time off school," said the first woman.

Thomas? thought Amira. *Oh, no. It must have been Kathleen who passed on.*

THAT EVENING, there was a happy reunion of all in the Dementia Unit dance class, although it seemed the first meeting for most of the participants. Afterwards, Amira and Gabriel walked to the hospital car park. Gabriel shuddered in the biting night air.

Amira took his hand and said, "Thomas's friend, Kathleen, has passed on."

"How terrible," said Gabriel. "Was she ill?"

"I don't think so," said Amira. "It was very sudden."

"How is Thomas?" asked Gabriel.

"Not good," said Amira. "I will go and see him when he has gotten over the initial shock."

"I think it's time for you to come home," she added.

Gabriel looked solemn and then nodded.

"I'll get my things and be about twenty minutes behind you," he said.

"That will be long enough to warm the house up," said Amira.

And, just like that, Gabriel was back home.

PART II
THE MIDDLE CIRCLE

DARNALL

CURIOSITY SHOP

CHAPTER 34
NOT DEAD YET

In Darnall:

Two months had passed. It was still winter, but no one in Gabriel and Amira's Dementia Unit dance class was cold. Everyone was hot and pumping jive.

The class had come to an equilibrium of its own accord. Gabriel was given notes from the "proper" dance instructors, although somewhat begrudgingly. The notes were enough to provide a loose direction, and Wolfgang and Madeline would demonstrate the technical elements of each dance for anyone interested. Although Madeline's mind could not remember the technique, her body remembered perfectly well the movements she had practised for so many years.

Lacking technical knowledge, Gabriel and Amira decided to transfer the feeling of each dance and give their students an immersive experience. All that meant was turning the music up and dancing enthusiastically with the class members in, more or less, the appropriate style. Gabriel would yell out encouragement and random advice above the music.

"Keep going. You're doing great. Jive is meant to be fun. Have fun, folks. Let's go. Go, go, go."

Everyone loved it, and they did have fun.

Sometimes, he added, "We're not dead yet. Keep those legs moving."

That was always greeted with peals of laughter. It was a fresh joke to most each time they heard it. Even the staff didn't seem to tire of the joke. Some who joined the frivolities felt more alive than they did for the rest of their week. Amira was the only one who would look sideways at Gabriel when he repeated the joke, yet again, to which he would say, "I'm on a winner."

When Gabriel and Amira got to the car, Gabriel said, "It's so nice to drive only two minutes home instead of forty-five."

This week, they had moved into a Darnall apartment owned by the college. Gabriel was offered more work and the use of one of the apartments. They both felt it would be a positive move and would save Gabriel a lot of travel time.

Farkas and Ide had come to a workable childcare arrangement. Farkas was only working at Erdo's farm when Ide wasn't working at the hospital. Amira no longer needed to care for Lan-Lan.

Although he didn't say it, Gabriel was glad to live in neutral territory. As much as he felt welcomed into Amira's home, it was her house, not their house. *Welcome* is not the same as *belonging*.

He wasn't eager to return to Waldmeer but said to Amira, "You go visit whenever you want."

'I'll try and settle here," said Amira.

Gabriel looked at her, unconvinced that she would so easily leave her Waldmeer roots, smiled, and said, "It will work out."

CHAPTER 35
LISTENING

I n Waldmeer:

Thomas never returned to school. After Kathleen's passing, he took two weeks off. He had already been away from school for the preceding two weeks on holiday with her. By the end of a month away, he met up with his deputy in the cafe.

"I hear you have been doing a fine job, Dennis," said Thomas, who had heard that his much younger deputy had stepped up to the plate commendably.

"Happy to help," said Dennis.

Of course, Dennis was also happy to further his career, but it was a balance.

"I hope you are feeling better," added Dennis.

Thomas didn't address whether he felt better but said, "I have made some important decisions. Before meeting with you, I went to the real estate office to put my house on the market."

The real estate agent was a friend of Thomas's and reminded him of the morning Kathleen came in to say she was putting her holiday house up for sale. He then regretted saying it.

"You are doing such a good job at school," said Thomas to Dennis, "that I don't see why you can't continue to do so. I don't need to fulfil the rest of my obligation before retiring."

Dennis went to object, but Thomas stopped him.

"I have had a great run, and I am thrilled to see you growing into a bigger role."

"Where will you go once your house is sold?" asked Dennis.

"I am in the process of lining something up," said Thomas. "The old Darnall Arcade is for sale, and I am talking with the appropriate parties."

"What on earth would you do with that old building?" asked Dennis. "Does anyone even go there anymore?"

Darnall had two arcades. One was the newer, larger one with a bright tiled walkway, supermarket, and thriving, well-appointed shops. The other was the relatively forgotten, old arcade.

One of the shops took up three shop fronts. It had been a sewing school for twenty years. Across from the sewing school was the Curiosity Shop, which had been there much longer than the sewing school. It was full of old books, crockery, and war trinkets.

Strangely, the other four businesses in the arcade all had something to do with healing or alternative health. There was Holistic Healing, Darnall Health Foods and Natural Medicines, Alternative Health and Well Being Naturopathic Clinic, and Darnall Arcade Therapies.

It was strange because one would have thought that a town like Darnall would not have had that many healing businesses. It was also odd that they were all next door to each other, competing for a limited customer base. Although the arcade was quiet, the businesses had been there for some time, so someone was supporting them.

"I'm going to use one of the shops myself," said Thomas, "and educate people about things that will be useful to them."

Dennis wondered what the "things of use" were but didn't ask.

After hesitating, Thomas added, "I would like to form some sort of community with the existing shops and see where it leads."

"That's brave," said Dennis.

He imagined that more things could go wrong with Thomas's plan than could go right.

"I mean... entrepreneurial," corrected Dennis.

"It's not entrepreneurial," said Thomas. "It's listening."

CHAPTER 36
FRESH AIR

In Darnall:

Gabriel and Amira's apartment was fresh and light. The lounge room window had a partial view of the meandering river that ran through Darnall. Many of their neighbours were also staff from the college.

Although the apartment block was new, it was on the grounds of the original old home, which preceded the college. The original house was a large, double-storey building needing renovation and was currently unoccupied.

Someone in Waldmeer told Amira that, at one stage, the old house was owned by her four great-aunts and their mother. The sisters were Rose, Evanora, Melba, and Pearl, from youngest to oldest.

By the time Gabriel and Amira had moved into their Darnall apartment, Thomas had moved into a rented flat on a nearby street next to the river. It was a pleasant place with a pretty courtyard and outlook. He did not want to put money into buying another house or renting a large one.

Besides, all his eggs were going into the arcade. Not entirely by choice, he was having a clean start.

Kathleen's passing had a profound and irrevocable impact on him. He already knew what it was like to lose a long-term partner. That, in itself, was impactful enough. Now, he knew what it was like to lose someone you love. He could neither return to school, his house of decades, nor his identity of equally as long.

It was a breath of fresh air to walk down the main street of Darnall and not be greeted by every second person as the principal of Waldmeer State Secondary School.

Although the loss of identity was disturbing and, at times, frightening, its retention would have been worse. He was determined to pursue an updated identity and direction and hoped, by God's grace, to find it.

It didn't take Thomas long to realise he had a neighbour he already knew. Grace lived a few houses away from him. Harry and Mary (Grace and Joe's twins) went to Waldmeer State Secondary School. They had been in the same year level as Maria. Some years back, Grace had been seriously ill. After a trip to Eraldus, she had returned to Waldmeer well. She credited her recovery to Amira (or Maria as she was called in those days). Grace and Joe then separated, and Grace came to live in Darnall while Joe stayed on the dairy farm outside Waldmeer.

After seeing Grace a few times, Thomas told her about his arcade venture.

"I know it doesn't look much now," said Thomas, "but I can do something with it."

"I'm sure you can," said Grace, who was always gracious and true to her name.

After reflection, she added, "I have quite an association

with that arcade. I have been involved with the sewing school for years and have even considered buying it at times. I wanted to do something different with it, but I was never quite sure what."

Thomas listened with interest.

"The peculiar old Curiosity Shop across the walkway from the sewing school was owned by some sisters who lived in the original house on the college grounds," said Grace. "Maybe, it is still in that family. I believe those sisters are Amira's great aunts, although none of them is living now."

"Is that so?" said Thomas. "Amira and Gabriel have recently moved into the college apartments."

"Really?" said Grace. "Amira is here in Darnall? How wonderful. I will see her and ask her if she knows who owns the Curiosity Shop."

Thomas and Grace looked at each other and couldn't help feeling a trail of excitement running through their veins. Something was going to happen, and they both wanted to be counted in.

MAKE-OVERS
AND MOVE-ONS

CHAPTER 37
DECORATING SKELETONS

I n *Waldmeer:*

Amira walked along the main street of Waldmeer, greeted the locals, and looked into the shop windows to see if anything had changed. It was her first visit back since moving to Darnall.

"Hello," said a lady outside the Opportunity Shop.

Amira didn't recognise the woman but, on closer inspection, realised it was Amelia.

"You look so different," said Amira.

"Yes," said Amelia proudly. "It's all because of fabulous Mirko Merven. He's magic."

Mirko had recently set up a hairdressing and beauty salon in Darnall. He had a well-known salon in the city but had a midlife crisis and consequent sea/tree change. He considered Waldmeer for his salon, but his business sense prevailed, and the larger, busier town of Darnall won. He brought his most successful program, *Makeover in the Middle with Merven the Magician.*

Everything about Amelia's appearance had been

updated and improved. Gone was the frumpy, tired, and boring Amelia. She was ten kilos lighter. Her blow-dried, newly-coloured hair had a tasteful, trendy cut. Her stylish, pricey clothes were flattering to her redefined figure.

Amira wondered why Amelia's face looked so much younger, but then realised that she must have opted for Mirko's heavy-duty program of Botox and cosmetic fillers. There was no doubt that she looked much better on the outside. However, for all her effort, she looked sad and isolated.

Amira coloured her own hair (these days, there was enough grey to warrant colouring it), but that was the extent of her beauty regime. She felt that beauty was predominantly an internal affair.

Once, she visited with Mullum-Mullum a place in the other dimensions, where the residents were skeletons. They spent an inordinate amount of time and money on decorating their skeletal bodies, never realising that they were ignoring the vital, life-giving part of themselves.

I suppose, thought Amira, *self-love is a process. If a physical overhaul brings more freedom, creativity, and self-worth, it is part of that process. If it doesn't do that, then it is only decorating skeletons.*

CHAPTER 38
LINKS

"You look great," said Amira to Amelia. "You have changed so much that I had trouble recognising you."

Amelia looked pleased. She was easily flattered.

"My friend, Farkas, told me about Mirko," said Amelia. "They are both worth their weight in gold."

Amelia seemed to have forgotten that Farkas had introduced Amira to her not long ago.

"He has just moved house back into his old place on the hill," said Amelia, pointing up the hill behind them.

"Who?" said Amira with surprise. "Farkas?"

"Yes," said Amelia.

Verloren must have gone ahead and sold her house, thought Amira.

Although neither Farkas nor Amira could remember it, that house was where they had spent time together as garden spirits before coming to Waldmeer in human form. When Farkas arrived in Waldmeer as a man, he inherited the house and had a strong bond with it ever since.

"With his family?" queried Amira.

"What family?" responded Amelia.

Amira had not spoken to Ide since she had finished looking after baby Lan-Lan. She assumed that Ide had been busy with her baby, work, and Farkas. Ide had been busy with the former, but, as it turned out, not with Farkas.

Although Ide and Farkas had reached a workable child-care arrangement, they had not reached a workable relationship arrangement. Farkas didn't want to return to the relationship. His heart wasn't in it anymore. He felt terrible about hurting Ide, but told himself she would have no trouble finding a suitable mate when she wasn't quite as busy with child raising.

Ide had already grieved a lot about Farkas, and moving on didn't take her too long. Her sweet, trusting approach to life had invariably served her well. She kept her eyes open and her heart soft, accepting what stood before her each day, which saved her a lot of pain.

What Ide did not foresee was that the end of her relationship with Farkas would also mark the end of her closeness to Amira. It was not by either's intentional design. Their lives had been closely linked, and as one changed, so did the other.

CHAPTER 39
RETURN OF THE BIRDS

I*n Darnall:*

One sunlit morning in Darnall, Amira made an interesting discovery. Behind the bushes in their apartment's courtyard was a dilapidated fence backing onto the grounds of the original estate. In the middle of the fence was a broken gate. It led into an overgrown garden.

Although the garden was neglected, Amira instantly liked it. The winter sun seemed to shine more brightly as she made her way along the paths, tangled with all manner of abandoned plants. There must have been hundreds of roses. The climbing ones had clambered unrestrained over and through everything. They had innumerable buds waiting for their time to perform. The undisturbed oasis also had a great collection of birds within its safe walls. A majestic bird of prey perched on the uppermost branch of the grandest tree. It was Aquilla, Mullum-Mullum's wedge-tailed eagle.

"How are you enjoying your new residence?" asked Mullum-Mullum, who had been waiting for Amira to become aware of his presence on a bench.

"How lovely to see you," said Amira. "We have only been here a little while, but everything is going well. Gabriel is happy."

Mullum-Mullum smiled.

"Do you like your great aunt's roses?" he asked.

"I love them," said Amira. "Which of my great aunts looked after the garden?"

"Rose, of course," said Mullum-Mullum.

Rose had left her Eraldus house to Amira some years ago. Erdo, the forest mystic, had told Amira that Rose was a spiritually powerful woman. As Rose often visited the Eraldus house in spirit form, Amira had realised that. Since selling that house, Amira had not felt her great aunt around again.

"We have a different plan for you now that you are in Darnall," said Mullum-Mullum.

Amira looked at him quizzically.

"We do not want you to continue your professional healing practice here," he said.

"Oh, I assumed I would be," said Amira.

"No," said Mullum-Mullum. "We want you to come to the rose garden every morning, and I will tell you what we would like you to do each day."

"Really?" said Amira, thinking that gave a very undefined structure to the day.

"You are advanced enough, by now," said Mullum-Mullum, "to not need the normal structures that humans find helpful."

"What will I tell Gabriel that I am doing?" asked Amira. "He will worry if he thinks I am doing nothing."

Amira half-smiled and continued, "Or, at least, nothing reasonably conventional."

"No, he won't," said Mullum-Mullum, "Every time the thought enters his mind of what you are doing, he will listen to another thought that will tell him you know what you are doing, and he needn't be concerned about it."

"Okay," said Amira. "If you say so."

"You do not want to burden Gabriel by telling him things that would serve no beneficial purpose," said Mullum-Mullum. "He trusts you. That's all that is needed."

In the same way that Lucy and Lenny, Maria's parents, had a grounding effect on her, Gabriel had a grounding effect on Amira. Perhaps that was why Amira never saw him in the other worlds. Gabriel valued this world and felt that this was where the action was. He liked food and sex, going places, and interacting with people. He was a man of Earth, albeit a good one. He reminded Amira to be a human.

"While you are coming to see me in the rose garden," said Mullum-Mullum, "you will not travel anywhere at night. So, sleep well."

Aquilla gave a loud squawk, indicating that his master was about to leave.

"One last thing," said Mullum-Mullum. "You may have noticed that you are being called Amira, not Vera or Lady Faith, as you are called in Long Hill and the Outer Circle. That is because Amira is your Earth name, and the Middle Circle is Earth."

CHAPTER 40
ONE STITCH AT A TIME

I t took quite a lot of organising and reorganising, but finally, Thomas had a full stable of shop tenants in the Darnall Arcade. He wanted to use one of the shops himself, but all four healing and alternative health businesses wished to stay put and had substantial leases.

The rent was minimal to accommodate the ageing arcade and the low-income businesses. It was so low that the Curiosity Shop, which had a very long lease, was still there even though it had been closed for years. The estate of the sisters who owned it stipulated that only a family member was to take it over.

Of course, Thomas immediately thought of Amira as they were her great aunts. After consultation with Mullum-Mullum and Teresa, Amira returned to Thomas with a proposal.

"Teresa and I will take over the Curiosity Shop," said Amira. "She has recently employed a local boy, Dayne, to help her in the Waldmeer bookshop and will be able to come to Darnall a few days each week."

"Will you run a healing practice from it?" asked Thomas.

"No," said Amira. "It will remain a book and curiosity shop. There are enough healers in the arcade already. We want something to grow organically from what is already in my great aunts' shop. That takes time."

Amira raised her eyebrows slightly and said, "As the rent is so cheap, we have time on our side."

Thomas felt that time wasn't on his side. He wanted to get his educational business up and running, but was unsure how or what to do. In the end, he and Grace took over the sewing school, the only available shop. It had a huge table in the middle of the floor and a poster saying,

Beautiful things come together one stitch at a time.

Thomas said he would use the table for meetings and sessions. Grace would run sewing and craft classes for income. She had budding plans for using the space in a healing manner. It would have a simple beginning—offering delicious, homemade cakes and tea and a sympathetic, listening ear. When we transform into a whole, healthy, and soulful being, we automatically want to help others do the same thing, as it strengthens and accelerates our transformation.

It wasn't a particularly easy partnership between Grace and Thomas. Thomas thought Grace was kind but weak, and Grace thought Thomas was delusional from too many years of being the principal. What they did not realise, and would not have wanted to know, was that the future success of their healing and business venture was intimately connected with their achieving an authentic bond with each other.

When Amira told Mullum-Mullum about Grace and Thomas, he said, "Perfect. Grace spent too many years obliging her ex-husband. Now, she is ready to learn what it means to value her abilities and talents. Thomas does not realise the strength of Grace's growing inspiration. He thinks only his ability and talent can turn the shop into what he dreams of. Grace must learn that everything truly worthwhile requires courage, and Thomas must learn who he is."

CHAPTER 41
RIGHT NOW

Amira spent most afternoons rummaging through the great jumble of books and paraphernalia in the Curiosity Shop. There was no hurry, so she would sit on the floor with a pile of dusty books and read. Sometimes, she would feel her Great-Aunt Rose directing her to certain books.

She got into business gear when Teresa was there, and started cleaning and doing whatever else Teresa instructed. Amira let Teresa be the boss. Teresa was a businesswoman. Amira wasn't.

One afternoon, through the dirty shop window, Teresa saw Bryan walking arm-in-arm with his new girlfriend, Leanne. Bryan hadn't yet realised who had taken over the shop. Amira saw him too and looked at Teresa with concern.

"It's alright," said Teresa. "I already know about her. She's a nice woman."

Leanne was everything one would say about a "nice" person. She was pretty and fashionably dressed in a quiet, understated way. She had an equally pleasant and attractive nature in a quiet, understated way. There was nothing about her that was offensive or objectionable.

"He doesn't love her," said Teresa. "He never will."

"I know," said Amira.

"I hear that he is drinking a lot," said Teresa with a frown.

"It's pain relief," said Amira

"I don't feel jealous of Leanne," said Teresa, "even though you would think I would. Who would want to fall in love with a man who loves someone else?"

"People often take whatever they can get," said Amira, "hoping it will become more."

"It's sad," said Teresa, "and infuriating. Can't he say sorry?"

"Bryan has two voices inside him," said Amira. "One is the better one—stable, amiable, trustworthy, honest, and warm. The other is the one that he is listening to now. The one that gets drunk, refuses to apologise, disregards the position he is putting another person in, and is proud and intractable. We all have different voices within us. We must choose which will get our attention. If we chose something else last week, yesterday, or a minute ago, it doesn't matter. We can make another choice... right now."

MAGIC MEN AND WOMEN

CHAPTER 42
OM MANI PADME HUM

In Waldmeer:

Farkas pulled his hood on and ran for Ide's front porch in the storm. He was picking up baby Lan-Lan.

Ide had been able to keep the house that she and Farkas had jointly owned, at least for now. The main elder of the Clinkers decided to rent Ide's large front room. He used it for meetings and private sessions and occasionally slept there.

His tribe name was Salt, although Ide's teenage son Christopher had always called him Magic Man. That is the name that stuck in Farkas's mind. Salt was an elder, but he was far from elderly. At seventy, he could run through the forest almost as fast as the young Clinker men and could certainly outwit them.

As Farkas made for the steps, he heard chanting through the windows.

Om mani padme hum.
Om mani padme hum.
Om mani padme hum.

He had heard their chanting before. It meant something about purification on the spiritual path, but all the Clinkers seemed to say it meant something different.

It was a traditional Buddhist mantra. The Clinkers were not Buddhists but had no qualms about taking whatever appealed to them from any tradition. They were not proud in that way.

Farkas thought they also seemed to have no qualms about taking whatever else they wanted. He already knew about Salt renting Ide's front room and wasn't entirely supportive of the idea, but his support was neither sought nor taken into account.

While waiting for Lan-Lan, Farkas looked through the partially open lounge room door. He could see Sri and Gloria from Vibes, the yoga studio. He saw other Waldmeer townsfolk, probably brought along by Sri and Gloria. As Ide greeted Farkas, Salt glanced in their direction with calm, clear eyes. They were calm, but there was a streak of something else in them.

What is it? thought Farkas. *Fierceness.*

Fierceness combined with a calm, determined mindset is a powerful tool. Farkas felt that he would not be easily getting near Ide again.

"How's Magic Man going?" Farkas asked Ide.

Hearing the tone in his voice, Ide said defensively, "He's fine. Leave him alone."

Farkas looked at Ide. She had bare feet and a long, flowing skirt. Her hair was loose and looked wilder than usual. He wasn't thrilled at the thought of his son being raised by a Clinker mother.

"Brother," a voice said from behind.

Farkas turned to see Salt holding out a hand. Sensing the tension in the hallway, Salt decided to intervene.

"You are welcome any time you wish," said Salt genuinely.

"Thanks," said Farkas. "I've got Lan-Lan now."

He walked back to the car, covering his baby's head with his jacket.

CHAPTER 43
MAC ENTERPRISE

I*n Darnall:*

"Who is that elderly lady with the long, white hair and walking stick who comes to your morning teas?" asked Teresa of Grace.

"She said her name is Rose," said Grace.

"Where does she live?" asked Teresa.

"I'm not sure," said Grace. "I presume somewhere in Darnall. It must be within walking distance."

They would see her slowly shuffling up the hill. However, they would not see her again anywhere around town.

There was something unusual about Rose. She didn't do or say anything unusual, but whenever she was around, everything worked well. She made a point of sitting next to Grace at the morning teas and looked encouragingly at her. The morning teas were going well. Not only did women come, but they sometimes brought their husbands and adult children with the promise of Grace's yummy baking.

Although Thomas generally didn't take any notice of the

morning teas, today, he did. He had trouble getting people to sign up for his MacArthur Enterprise Educational and Life Improvement Courses. He knew his courses were good, but he couldn't break through the barrier of getting the Darnall townsfolk to commit.

"I have an idea," said Thomas to Grace when all her visitors had left except Rose, who was sitting unassumingly. "Why don't you invite your people to my courses and bring their families?"

"Alright," said Grace obediently.

Rose looked up and said, "I'm sure they would love to come and hear you speak, Grace."

Grace looked shocked at the thought of her speaking at Thomas's event. Thomas looked annoyed at Rose for putting the idea in Grace's head.

As Thomas could not be anything but inviting in the situation, he said, "Yes, of course, Grace. You must say something."

He then added, "Not too long."

With Rose's help, Grace worked out a simple, authentic message. The evening arrived, and Thomas, as expected, spoke impressively. He was an experienced motivational speaker and teacher. However, Grace's somewhat fumbling talk touched people's hearts. The sincerity of her desire to improve her life and to reach out to others along the way was undeniable. At one point, Thomas looked at the small audience and saw their attentive and moved expressions while Grace spoke. He felt humbled by it and reached for Grace's hand as she faltered. It gave Grace the courage to continue.

The following day, Thomas entered the shop and said to Grace, "I have a brilliant idea about the name of the Enterprise."

"It already has a name," said Grace, "MacArthur Enterprise."

"Mac and Mac Enterprise," said Thomas proudly.

"Mac and Mac?" queried Grace.

"Yes," said Thomas, pointing to himself and then to Grace. "MacArthur and Maclary; Mac and Mac."

Grace had kept her marital surname of Maclary. She had had it so long, and it was so intertwined with the business she had run with her husband, Maclary Dairy, that she couldn't see the point in changing it.

"Mac and Mac Enterprise," repeated Grace. "How about Mac and Mac and no Enterprise? It sounds more approachable."

And that is how Mac & Mac was born.

CHAPTER 44
DELICIOUS

As Bryan was ambling through Darnall Arcade, he saw the new sign above the old sewing school saying, *Mac & Mac*. Grace beckoned to him and pointed to her lemon and coconut cake. He had been a few years ahead of Grace's twins at school.

"How are you?" asked Grace. "Please have some cake. How are your parents?"

"Hmm, don't mind if I do," said Bryan.

He was always hungry from farm work. After a little chat, Grace asked Bryan if he knew that Teresa and Amira had taken over the Curiosity Shop opposite.

"No," said Bryan, turning to look.

Teresa had already seen him and was watching as much as was polite. She waved to him, and he waved back.

"Take this over to Teresa," said Grace, handing him a slice of cake.

It seemed more of a motherly order than a request. Bryan kissed Grace goodbye and walked the few steps to Teresa's shop.

"I have to get back to work," said Bryan to Teresa after a quick catch-up about nothing of much importance.

As he reached the door, he turned to Teresa and said, "It's nice to see you."

He wanted to add, *I miss you,* but didn't.

"I know you have moved on," said Teresa hesitantly, "but if you ever look back, I am ready to get married."

Bryan stood stock-still.

"You drive a hard bargain," continued Teresa, trying to smile, "but I guess you want the security of the commitment, or you did want it."

Bryan thought momentarily, stared at her piercingly, and said, "In Spring."

"At the Waldmeer Convent," said Teresa.

She added, "Family only."

It was a small concession for a big decision. Bryan smiled and walked out into the Arcade. Teresa made a cup of tea and sat down to eat Grace's cake. It was even more delicious than usual.

WINTER LIGHTS

CHAPTER 45
SUSPICIOUS ARRANGEMENTS

In Darnall:

Mullum-Mullum was not in the rose garden. Amira decided to walk up the back steps of the old house and look around the verandah.

Some dusty boxes and a few bits of dirty furniture were haphazardly pushed into a corner where they had remained for years. She spotted a small bookshelf and pulled out several yellowed books. Her eyes landed on a familiar green cover. It was *The Little Book of Healing*. On the inside of the cover was a sticker saying, *This book belongs to Rose Este*.

The book had long since ceased publication. Amira had given her precious copy to Thomas a few years ago. There was something quite peculiar about the little book. Amira didn't know if other people had the same experience, but she often seemed to read pages she had never seen before. As she had read the book many times and it wasn't long, she decided it must change its contents depending on what was needed. She put it in her pocket and returned to the apartment.

GABRIEL WAS AWAKE AND UP. He had been out late the night before. Unfortunately, he was frequenting the Darnall night-club with the Boys of Darnall. His behaviour would have told Amira even if he hadn't. He was disconnected; at least he was disconnected from her.

It wasn't just his absences that were the problem. When he was home, he was out of sorts and would start up with all manner of complaints: "It's too hot in here. Why have you got the heat up so high?" "It's too cold." "You know I don't like this," (pointing to some food he happily ate a few weeks ago.)

"The mentality of that group is not having a good effect on you," said Amira.

"I like the mentality," said Gabriel.

Amira turned away and rolled her eyes.

"Just because you act like an old lady," said Gabriel, "everybody else doesn't have to."

"I don't know about 'old'," said Amira quietly, "but there are a few too many 'ladies' around at the moment."

"What did you say?" said Gabriel. "I can't hear you."

"I said, 'What makes them any different to any hetero-male group that you find so stupid?'" replied Amira. "The college jocks fixated on their female counterparts or the old guys at the pub swooning over some woman's boobs. It's the same ridiculous, superficial mentality. How can it possibly make anyone happy?"

When it came to a rational argument, Gabriel had no hope against Amira. However, the thing about arguments is that they don't have to be rational, and usually they are not. They are all emotion.

"It's my life," said Gabriel.

He won, if one could call such a thing a win.

"If you think I'm so stupid, why are you even with me?" he added on his way out.

AMIRA RETURNED to the rose garden, hoping that Mullum-Mullum might be there now. He was.

"I feel sad," said Amira.

"I know," said Mullum-Mullum, taking her hand.

They walked around the garden slowly and silently.

"I'm tired of him hurting me," said Amira.

Mullum-Mullum pointed to one of his birds. They were always talking to him and telling him things.

"Do not assume," said Mullum-Mullum, "that someone else's ego can love you. It cannot. It does not even love the person it resides in. The limit of the ego's 'love' is to decide that you are a temporary ally, and thus it will protect you for the benefit of its own use. Only a soul can accept and return love. Everything else is manipulation. Fragile arrangements. They are, at best, suspicious and, at worst, vicious."

"That's not cheering me up," said Amira.

CHAPTER 46
ALL AROUND US

After work, Amira packed a small bag of clothes and left a note for Gabriel saying she would return to Waldmeer for a few days.

It was dark by the time she drove up her familiar home hill. The winter lights were on. Waldmeer had a high tourist population in summer, and a hill full of lights in summer would be spotted with only a few lights during the long winter evenings. The locals knew who was home by the familiar lights of full-time residents. They would have known that Amira was home.

Walking to the shops the next morning, she saw Farkas and baby Lan-Lan in the park.

"I saw your lights on last night," said Farkas.

She didn't feel much like talking, so she let him talk.

"Did you know that Magic Man is at Ide's?" asked Farkas.

"No," said Amira. "I suppose Ide *is* a Clinker. It will probably be good for her to have him there."

"I think he's interested in her," said Farkas.

Amira thought about that for a moment. *Farkas is intu-*

itive about such things, Ide is an old soul, and Salt is a free spirit, so it is a possibility.

"People need many more things in life," said Amira, "than a same-age, same-life-experience, comfortable companion."

"Not to state the obvious," said Farkas, "but there is a thirty-year age difference."

Amira shrugged. She didn't care how many years' age difference there was. Today, instead of positively affecting Farkas, he was making her state of mind worse.

I need to fix myself up, she thought.

"I'll see you later," she said. "Goodbye, little Lan-Lan."

She headed for the beach. With a thick coat, woollen hat, big scarf, and gloves, the bitter wind was a clearing agent rather than a cold, disagreeable enemy. She recalled this morning's offering from *The Little Book of Healing,*

Love is its own reward. We do not have to worry about what other people think about us. We can never feel alone or isolated when we understand that it is impossible for love to leave our side. Love is all around us.

She kept walking and repeated silently, *Love is all around us.*

Feeling much improved, she stopped walking and said out loud, "I'm not going back."

PERSONAL BAROMETER

CHAPTER 47
CAT FIGHTS

In Darnall:

You're a jealous cow," screeched the black cat to the tabby cat cornered on the branch's thin end.

"The Great One is not jealous of the gods you make," said the tabby with the tenacity of a worthy opponent, "and neither am I."

Gabriel heard the commotion of the fighting cats not far from his window in the middle of the night. As it was not subsiding, he got up in exasperation, pulled on clothes at the end of the bed, and went outside to search for the source of the untimely disturbance.

He shone a torch into the tree, but neither cat moved. The tabby couldn't move, and the black one refused to. He threw a stick towards the black cat, who conceded temporary defeat and retreated. The tabby could then escape.

"Have your arguments elsewhere," Gabriel yelled at the cats, probably waking up the neighbours as much as the arguing cats.

~

AMIRA HAD HARDLY BEEN BACK to Darnall in the last few weeks. Teresa had been taking most of the shifts at the Curiosity Shop, and Amira had been helping the new shop assistant, Dayne, in the Waldmeer shop. He was a delightful twenty-two-year-old. Home-schooled by a religious family, he was unusually polite, hardworking, and good.

As Amira wasn't travelling to Darnall, she wasn't meeting Mullum-Mullum in the old rose garden. However, since being back in Waldmeer, her night travels had recommenced, although they were confined to the Waldmeer/Darnall environs.

She had witnessed the catfight and Gabriel's intervention in her travels. She knew who the cats were. The menacing black cat was Great Aunt Evanora, and the tabby was Evanora's little sister, Rose. Evanora was rather fond of taking cat form. Rose followed suit to keep an eye on her.

Amira had also been night-travelling inside the old house and had seen the four sisters and their mother, Mercy, at various stages of their family life.

Rose had a lot of light. Evanora had a lot of dark. The two older girls, Melba and Pearl, were more conventional in temperament, interests, and life direction. Unlike Rose and Evanora, they both married and had children.

There was often tension in the family home. It tended to come from Evanora. Rose would try to counteract it.

Evanora was particularly jealous of other people's relationships. She desperately wanted to be loved, but was poisonous in relationships and quickly destroyed them. Out of bitterness, she actively sought to destroy the happiness of others.

As the cat ladies were parting company on the evening of Gabriel's intervention, Amira heard Evanora hiss at Rose, "If Amira returns to Gabriel, I will kill him."

She woke in a sweat and remembered that Evanora had killed her adored German shepherd back in Eraldus a few years ago.

Now she had two problems.

The first was the broken-down state of her relationship with Gabriel.

The second was the dangerous energy working against its healing.

CHAPTER 48
SOMEONE IS MISSING

When Amira walked into the Dementia Unit for the dance class, she could hear one of her class participants complaining to the carer at the desk. "My mother said she would come and see me. She hasn't been for ages. I miss her, and I think something must be wrong. Can you ring her?"

She was clearly upset. She would have been in her early nineties. The carer was trying to ignore her. It was probably the twentieth time she had come to the desk that day. An experienced carer came around the corner and summed up the situation in the twinkling of an eye.

"I'm so sorry, Mavis," he said. "I forgot to tell you. Your Mum rang a little while ago. She's on her way."

The carer at the desk looked at him with raised eyebrows.

"Thank you so much," said Mavis, who was already relaxing. "I was worried. I haven't seen her in a while and wanted to make sure she was alright."

Mind you, "a while" would have been thirty years.

The carer patted her back and said, "She's fine. You go with Amira and enjoy your dancing."

Taking her hand, Amira and Mavis waltzed into the class.

Last week, Gabriel took the class on his own, and Amira took this one on her own. Both times, the Dementia Unit residents kept saying, "Someone is missing." However, they couldn't remember who it was. Amira didn't know how Gabriel went, but her class hadn't gone particularly well.

There were only a few weeks left of the classes. The Psychology Department was concluding the Dementia Unit test program. Amira decided to take the class to the city to see the ballet.

CHAPTER 49
SWIRLING HEMS

The ballet company had a popular pas de deux couple, Clayton and Kristel. Clayton was a vibrant, outgoing dancer whose giant leaps and entertaining stage presence won the hearts of his followers some years back.

Kristel was a newer star. Her usual demeanour was far from that of a star. She was reserved and preferred her own company. She was the opposite of self-promoting. It was a wonder that she was given the prestigious lead role, except that she could be captivating when she danced. She had a purity about her, and it translated into a fragile, enchanting beauty in dancing.

The Directors of the ballet company were not unanimous in supporting Kristel. Many preferred the more dominant, exciting dancing of some of the fiercer female students. If it were not for the insistence of the most senior director, Kristel would not have been given the lead role.

"Kristel has dancing in her," said the director quite adamantly.

His fellow directors wondered what he thought the other students had in them.

"Our job is to protect it," he continued. "If we try to mould it, we may destroy it. Just protect it and make it feel safe. It will come out. You will see."

"And then," he added with a smile, "everyone will thank us for giving them a gift."

Amira had to keep her people quiet, somewhat like keeping a preschooler quiet. It helped that they were attending the matinee, and there were children in the audience. The ballet's tolerance for audience noise was higher than usual.

Clayton and Kristel's partnership had its ups and downs. If Clayton pushed too hard or ignored Kristel's gentle presence, the duet became unbalanced. Kristel would underperform and look less than the corps de ballet, and Clayton would look like a self-absorbed show-off. If they got it right, Kristel forgot herself and became entrancing, and Clayton became the strong, brilliant dancer he was. Isn't it the task of art to bring out our best selves?

Today, they got it right. They were so together and absorbed in the dance that they became much more than their small, individual selves. The audience felt equally included in the magic of the moment. Everyone, including the children and the Dementia Unit folk, was spellbound.

After the performance, two of Amira's ladies said they fancied the good-looking male dancers with their bare, toned bodies. Amira smiled. The ladies often forgot their age and had no concept of their appearance.

"We want to go backstage and meet them," said one of the ladies who thought they had a fighting chance.

So, they did. The ladies flirted their petticoats off, and the boys, to their credit, got on board and flirted back with a vengeance.

Remembering the Dementia Unit dance class, one lady told the dancers, "We have our own training."

Amira nodded in affirmation.

After consideration, one of the men said, "The famous actress, Rita Moreno, is still doing it at eighty-five, so you keep swirling those hems too."

The dancer lived with his grandmother, who fancied a twirl or two, and that is how he knew about Rita Moreno and swirling hems. The women looked momentarily confused as to why Rita Moreno, at eighty-five, had anything to do with them.

"We have to see our other girlfriends now," the dancer said, kissing their hands. "Keep swirling those hems, ladies."

On the long drive back to Darnall in the country bus, everyone was content and talked about the ballet and the gorgeous dancers until they forgot where they had been. The memory of the event may have drifted into the ether, but the feeling of beauty and hope remained inside them.

CHAPTER 50
LOSERS

On Amira's next shift at the Curiosity Shop, she stopped by the old rose garden, hoping to see Mullum-Mullum. He was waiting for her.

"You have to stay out of the game," said Mullum-Mullum. "It's deadly, and no one ever wins. Everyone is a loser. Even seeming wins are short-lived and have the taste of bitterness mixed in with the satisfaction of personal gain."

He bent to touch some of the early flowering bulbs, brave little things announcing the way to warmer days.

"The ego is exclusive by nature," he continued. "While the spirit seeks to include, the ego is unashamedly manipulative in its culling of people. The soul does not see people in terms of what it can gain. It seeks to share."

Pulling out some weeds that were choking a clump of freesias, Mullum-Mullum said, "The ego is extremely changeable. Constantly guarding against attack, its perceptions and feelings are ever-shifting. This creates unhappiness."

"It saddens me to see it," said Amira.

"It is how humans learn," said Mullum-Mullum. "The more they veer away from their true nature, the more unhappy they feel. When they align with their better self, they feel happy again. And so the process continues until the spaces between happiness are not as long and arduous."

NARROW LANE

CHAPTER 51
NEXT DOOR

Night travels (inter-dimensional):

"We have taken matters into our own hands," said Mullum-Mullum to Amira. "We had concerns about Gabriel's safety regarding Evanora. There is no need for you to be worried. However, we ask that you not see him unless instructed to do so."

Mullum-Mullum gazed into the distance. Amira couldn't see where he was looking. Nor could she see anything around him. Usually, if Amira saw Mullum-Mullum in her night travels, she saw him in the setting of the Darnall rose garden. However, for some reason, tonight, he seemed to be standing in a blank space with no distinguishing features.

"I guess," sighed Amira, "Gabriel hasn't suffered enough yet."

"We'd be out of business," laughed Mullum-Mullum, "if people were done with their suffering."

THAT'S STRANGE, thought Amira when she woke up. *What have they done? And why is Mullum-Mullum not talking to me from the rose garden?*

She was relieved that he had decided to do something about Evanora. It was concerning that Gabriel lived next door to her. Her consolation was that he also lived next door to Rose. Even more comforting, Mullum-Mullum was in the estate's garden.

Amira soon discovered what they had done. On the way to the Curiosity Shop the following day, she pulled up at the estate.

To her shock, it was gone.

No dilapidated house, forgotten garden, old roses, awakening bulbs. The area had been raised for redevelopment.

She walked around the flattened block to see if she could sense her four great-aunts and their mother. Nothing.

She looked up to see if there were any birds. Not only were there no birds, but all the trees on the estate were gone.

There were not even any cats.

CHAPTER 52
REPLANTING

*I*n the Leleks:

After the Darnall estate had been demolished, there was no longer a physical place to meet Mullum-Mullum. Feeling that she needed some help, Amira went to Erdo in the Leleks. Erdo was a step down from Mullum-Mullum in the spiritual hierarchy, but he was still an advanced teacher.

She crossed the rickety walking bridge, but Erdo wasn't in his usual spot by the lake. Instead, Farkas was standing there. It was somewhat out of context.

"What are you doing here?" asked Amira.

"Well, that's a fine hello," said Farkas. "Erdo told me to bring you back to the farm."

They walked the half-hour track further into the forest, mostly in silence. Amira was very interested in seeing Erdo's house and farm. She had never been there, and he hadn't even mentioned it all these years.

~

AT ERDO'S FARM:

"How long have you had the farm?" asked Amira.

"Oh, it just seems like yesterday," said Erdo.

Indicating the end of that topic, he ushered her into the lounge room. The room was warmed by a wood fire and had comfortable, homely furniture. It was the sort of lounge room where one feels instantly at home. Farkas turned to leave, but Erdo told him to stay.

"We are all on this journey together," said Erdo.

The look on Farkas's face suggested that he thought his journey was private, but he stayed anyway.

"Today, we are going to talk about change," said Erdo. "In my early years in the forest, I was married to Miya, who was originally my student. She was beautiful in every way. After seven years together, she told me she would leave her body. I suggested that there was no hurry. She replied, 'Right now, I am perfectly happy both on the inside and the outside.' The next evening, as we sat together, I looked over at her and saw that she had gone. She left her body as easily as taking off her clothes. She was twenty-nine."

Erdo got up and poked the fire.

"The yogis call it Mahasamadhi," he said. "It is consciously and intentionally leaving one's body and dissolving into the Infinite."

Farkas looked like he couldn't think of anything worse than *dissolving into the Infinite.* Amira couldn't help laughing.

"Don't worry, Farkas," she said, "I don't think you will be dissolving anytime soon."

Farkas couldn't see the humour in that. Amira looked out the window. It was winter, and the fields were bare. Soon, Erdo and Farkas would be preparing the soil for planting.

"Back to the here and now," said Erdo with a smile.

"Relationships are constantly changing. They have to be dealt with every day anew. You have to pay attention. It is painful if things take a turn for the worse, but it's a chance to see things differently. So that is a helpful pain."

"Why is your house number forty-five?" asked Amira on the way out. "There is no street, and there are no other houses."

"It was given by the Advisors of the Homeland when Miya returned to them. Numerologically, forty-five means *to put our efforts towards the things in life that enhance our highest self*."

"I will not be replanting crops in the coming spring," Erdo said to Farkas, "so I won't need you anymore. You will have other things to do back in Waldmeer."

"Do you need someone to take you back to the walking bridge?" he asked Amira.

"No thanks," said Amira. "I know the way."

CHAPTER 53
CROWDS

In Darnall:

The following week, Amira dropped books to the Curiosity Shop from Teresa's Waldmeer bookshop. As she approached, she saw that the Curiosity Shop was crowded.

That's good for business, she thought.

However, she found only Teresa in the shop when she got there.

"Where is everyone else?" asked Amira.

"What do you mean?" said Teresa. "I've only had a few visitors all morning."

Amira could see the crowd now and again from the corner of her eye.

Oh, my goodness, she thought. *It's my great-aunts. They have all moved into their old Curiosity Shop!*

It was dusk by the time Amira left the Curiosity Shop. She could see the fading sunset colours through the entrance door of the Darnall Arcade. Coming through the sliding door was an elderly lady with long, grey hair and a walking stick. It was the lady who had been helping Grace with her morning teas. Grace said her name was Rose. Amira assumed it was a manifestation of her Great Aunt Rose.

"We would like you to come to our meeting," said Rose kindly, but not leaving room for anything but a positive answer.

They walked a few streets and then turned into a lane that Amira had not been down before. At the bottom of the lane, they turned into another small street called Narrow Lane. They entered an ivy-clad building by its back door. Inside, there was an expectant but calm atmosphere.

The folk in the room were a mixture of Earth dwellers and inter-dimensional beings. The inter-dimensional ones included Mullum-Mullum, seated in the front row next to Lord Lan-Lan from Long Hill. Erdo was a few rows away with his sister Milyaket from the Homeland. The Head Gardener from the Garden of Garourinn was also in the small crowd, but the Master of Garourinn was not.

There were humans in the room, too. Amira vaguely recognised some of the faces as people she had crossed paths with at various times. She thought she saw Salt, the Clinker elder from the back hills of Waldmeer.

She felt that the inter-dimensional folk were there to support the humans.

About thirty individuals (human and inter-dimensional) were in the room, although there may have been many more invisible ones that Amira couldn't see. They were all waiting for someone to speak.

"For those of you visiting for the first time, my name is Advaitaguru," said a man who had appeared at the front. "You are very welcome."

Advaitaguru spoke in an unhurried but direct manner. His presence was simultaneously humbling and uplifting.

"Humans who are present," he said, "please try to practise these two points:

1. Do not like or dislike anyone. Share your love regardless of how it is received. Anyone who can receive it will do so. Many, of whom you are unaware, will benefit from it.

2. See yourself as a total person, not a partial person. Do not seek completion from other humans."

He paused to let the critical lessons sink into the memory of his human audience.

"You have the support of everyone in this room and many more," he continued, still speaking to the Earth dwellers. "Do not be disturbed by pains that come and go. Pick yourself up and take each pain as an important opportunity to progress. Forgive everyone who hurts you (they are suffering). Tell yourself that you will have a happy and blessed life. You are loved beyond anything you can currently perceive. Be brave. Do not fall asleep."

He raised his hand, and a light passed over the room. A mighty peace entered everyone's heart. The inter-dimensional beings began to fade and disappear. The remaining humans smiled at each other, nodded in acknowledgment, and left.

On the drive home to Waldmeer, Amira repeated Advaitaguru's words,

Share your love regardless of how it is received.
You will have a happy and blessed life.

She looked into the black night sky with its endless, radiant lights and thanked the Power behind all the other powers.

HANDSPUN

CHAPTER 54
BEST FRIEND

In Darnall:

Tonight was the last Dementia Unit dance class. Wolfgang was in fine form and had been talking nonstop.

"I like making a noise," he joked. "I should have been a politician. Do you know I come here every morning for breakfast with my Madeline?"

"That's devoted," said Gabriel.

"Dementia patients are a bit like drunks," said Wolfgang. "Some are sad drunks. Some are angry drunks. My Madeline is a happy drunk. I get more kisses and hugs when she sees me than all my married mates put together. I'm not convinced she always knows that it's me she's kissing, but I take it anyway."

At the end of the class, he said, "We will miss you both."

"Here's another kiss to add to your collection," said Amira, kissing him on the cheek.

Only Wolfgang would miss them because everyone else was unlikely to remember.

Perhaps that is a saving grace, thought Amira. *What we cannot remember, we do not grieve.*

Gabriel and Amira stood at the end of the long hospital corridor. Once they opened the outside door, it would be cold, and both would immediately head for their cars.

"How are you going?" asked Amira.

"Great," said Gabriel. "I'm great."

Amira saw a tiny ant pushing a crumb, much bigger than itself, over the expanse of the walkway.

He's a brave little soldier, she thought.

Telling herself that she had nothing more to lose, she said, "I'm not trying to hurt you, but much of the time, you act like I am."

Gabriel was not going to tolerate the conversation for long.

"You expect a great deal of loyalty," said Amira, "but your mind is so changeable that your loyalty is fragile."

Gabriel looked at her with a combination of hurt, anger, and indifference.

"Bye," he said, walking off.

"Don't worry, love," said a voice in the partial darkness. It was Wolfgang. "We're our own worst enemy." He looked back at the Dementia Unit and added, "We're also our own best friend."

CHAPTER 55
OPEN DOOR

"**W**here do you go with Rose?" asked Grace one afternoon while locking up her Darnall Arcade shop. It was not like Grace to ask a personal question uninvited.

"Would you like to come too?" answered Amira.

"If that is alright?" said Grace.

"You only had to ask," said Amira.

Each time Amira went to Advaitaguru's meetings, it was different. Sometimes, there were only a few participants. Other times, there were many. Sometimes, Amira knew many of those in the audience. Other times, she knew no one. It was always Advaitaguru speaking, although, on occasion, he stood out the front saying nothing. The meetings never lasted more than ten minutes or so.

In the beginning, Amira only went to the meetings when Rose met her at the sliding doors of the Darnall Arcade. However, after a few visits, she started walking there herself, down the side street, into Narrow Lane, and then into the back door of the ivy-covered building. When Amira and

Grace got to the entrance of the unmarked brick building, it wouldn't open.

"That's strange," said Amira. "It always opens."

She could hear people speaking inside, so she knew they were there.

"It's me," blurted out Grace as if she were exposing a long-held secret. "They won't let me in. I'm not good enough."

"Don't be ridiculous," said Amira with no sympathy.

Not knowing what else to do, she suggested, "Let's try again tomorrow."

On the way to Narrow Lane the next day, Amira said, "The way is not narrow. It's wide. Everyone is welcome. However, we must know that we are welcome, or we keep the door shut ourselves."

After a pause, she added, "There is no one better than you."

To Grace's delight, the door opened.

Afterwards, Amira asked, "How did you like the meeting?"

"I don't want to disappoint you," said Grace, "but I couldn't see or hear anything."

"You will," said Amira. "Probably, there are many things in that little room that *I* can't see or hear. They give us as much as we will take."

CHAPTER 56
HOMEMADE

Bryan and Teresa had happily settled back into their relationship. Both had been hurt, although neither had purposely hurt the other. They picked up the pieces, left behind the blame, and started again with their eyes forward.

"Bryan and I have been talking," said Teresa to Amira one morning in the Curiosity Shop. "As much as you and I love the old books and curiosity items that your great aunts kept in this shop, there is no future in it."

Amira loved sitting on the floor and rummaging through the yellowed books, but she knew that the current shop was not viable from a business point of view. Besides, she did not feel comfortable having her great-aunts come and go in spirit form. Wherever Evanora went, trouble was bound to follow. If the books and paraphernalia were gone, the sisters would likely be too.

"Bryan has been discussing an idea with his mother," said Teresa. "He feels there is a market for Clarice's hand-spun, homemade wool products."

Bryan's family farm was a mixture of sheep and cattle. The sheep were shorn once a year.

The workday started at 7.30 a.m. in the tin shed during the shearing season. The day was divided into four runs of two hours each. Smoko breaks and lunch punctuated the runs. The shearers were paid per sheep. Those who tallied more than two hundred sheep daily were known as gun shearers. The fastest shearer in the shed was the ringer.

After the shearers removed the wool from the sheep, the fleece was thrown onto the wool table, skirted, rolled, and classed. Then it was placed in an appropriate wool bin, pressed, and stored until transported.

Sometime during the second run of the day, Clarice would appear. The shearers would look at each other with a silent groan. They would never outright disrespect the boss's missus. Besides, she always brought a freshly baked cake with her.

Clarice watched the shearing with sharp eyes. She ensured that the floor was kept clean and that they did not throw the fleece onto oil patches. She pointed out repeatedly that they shouldn't do second cuts. She then picked out the best wool for her home projects.

As she walked back down the ramp of the shearing shed and headed for the farmhouse, the men smiled at each other and returned to their more manageable charges.

Back at the house, Clarice would get to work on her chosen wool—sorting, teasing, washing, drying, combing, and dying with natural colours. She had a great pile of used tea leaves to dye. She would spin the wool into yarn on her spinning wheel. Clarice said that spinning was the most calming thing she had ever done. It was meditative, though she would not use that word.

For the shop, the intention was to sell Clarice's skeins of naturally-dyed, hand-spun yarn. They would also sell products knitted by Clarice and some of the women from the Waldmeer Country Women's Association—baby moccasins, slippers, throws, cushions, toys, teddies, and an assortment of vests and jumpers. They were going to be discerning about what they sold. They wanted the shop to be classy and cultured, not a place for all the remnants that couldn't be sold at the country fairs.

One clever young lady in the C.W.A. was a talented weaver of wall hangings. She was the only young member of the group. Her name was Rachael. The older women mothered her, fussed over her, bossed her around, and taught her weaving traditions passed down from their mothers and grandmothers.

In return, she gave them her youthful energy and her spirited artistry. That artistry would provide the shop with an upmarket, vital edge. It only took a few weeks, and the Curiosity Shop became a vibrant and flourishing business with the new name of *Handspun*.

Box by box, Amira packed the old books and curiosity items and drove them to their new home, her bungalow. The bungalow hadn't been occupied since Gabriel used it as a country art studio several years ago. Much of his art equipment was still in it. Amira felt her four great aunts would follow their belongings to the bungalow. However, she was confident they wouldn't come into her Waldmeer house.

They can live in the bungalow until I work out what to do with them, thought Amira.

PROTECTION

CHAPTER 57
SWEET RUTHLESSNESS

I*n Darnall:*
As Amira walked out of Handspun, she bumped into Gabriel and some of the Boys of Darnall, who were taking a shortcut through the Arcade. The Boys included some women, two of whom were walking with the group today.

No one in that group was generally friendly towards Amira, although some were more polite than others. Gabriel, however, stopped to talk to her. Despite their problems, he did love Amira. Even if he didn't, he was not a rude person.

As he was talking, Amira could feel the eyes of one of the women boring into her back. It was Bridgette. She didn't live in Darnall. She was an artist like Gabriel and lived in the city.

"Hi, Bridgette," said Amira, turning to face her. "How are you?"

"Fine," said Bridgette, not returning the courtesy of asking how Amira was.

Not so easily deterred by Bridgette's barely veiled animosity, Amira asked where she was staying while in Darnall.

"At Gabriel's," said Bridgette with a smile at Gabriel. "It's always great to catch up with my lifelong friend. We go together. Don't we, Gabriel?"

Amira looked at Gabriel, who was silent. Bridgette was in her early thirties. She met him about ten years ago when she started her art career. Amira thought it wasn't exactly "lifelong" but was long enough. What it was "long enough" for was yet to be discerned.

"Let's go," said Gabriel to the group. "See you later, Amira."

As Amira got in her car to drive back to Waldmeer, she kept thinking about Bridgette.

What does she want from Gabriel? And why does she look at me with such competitive hatred?

Bridgette had a long-term boyfriend in the city, so Amira didn't feel she wanted a relationship with Gabriel. Perhaps, she had a different sort of proposition in mind. Whatever it was, she must have felt Amira was an enemy of her plans.

An attractive woman, Bridgette wore her short, blonde hair perfectly. She was the sort of woman that men tended to like. She was clever but didn't flaunt it. Men like that. She was also ambitious and manipulative, but hid it behind a pretty face and pleasant personality.

Sweet ruthlessness, thought Amira.

AMIRA APPROACHED the crossroads to Waldmeer.

The car in front stopped abruptly.

Having no time to brake, she swerved sharply, catching the back corner of the front vehicle.

Swinging around, she crashed into the side of the stationary vehicle.

After sitting there for a few moments, she wondered if she was still here. Not only was she *here,* but she seemed unharmed except for some bruising.

All in all, it was nothing for that sort of a crash.

Somewhat dazed, she looked out the window of her damaged car to the cows, who had returned to their munching.

Why? she asked herself.

And for the second time that day, she thought, *Sweet ruthlessness. Ruthless, indeed.*

CHAPTER 58
CALLING

In the city:

Amira was not the only one in the accident zone this week. Ide's fifteen-year-old son, Christopher, had been visiting his friend in the city and had broken his leg at the skate park. He was taken to the closest Emergency Department in one of the city's busiest public hospitals.

Ide was driving there from Waldmeer. Baby Lan-Lan had been dropped off at his dad's place. Being a nurse, Ide was used to hospitals. However, things are different when it is a family member. Also, Ide was used to the quiet, little country hospital in Waldmeer, not the hectic pace of a large inner-city hospital.

At least a broken leg is mendable, and it isn't anything worse, she reassured herself while navigating the country roads she knew so well.

Ide's city driving was not the best when all was well, let alone under stress. As she got closer to the hospital, she prayed, *Please, help Christopher to be okay. Help him manage the pain. Don't let him get too anxious. Help me find a suitable park. Tell all the right people to help us.*

She kept telling herself to calm down, or she wouldn't be able to see or hear any answers to her prayers. Finally, she found the hospital parking station, worked out the parking system, and then figured out how to navigate the walkways and lifts through the hospital. The hospital was a great conglomeration of buildings of different architecture. It had been extended over many years and joined in a seemingly incomprehensible system of tunnels and passages.

The Emergency Department was busy, clinical, and unpleasant. Sick people were unhappily sitting on chairs. Some were moaning or vomiting. Drug addicts, alcoholics, and mentally ill people walked up and down the aisles, yelling out random messages to the Gods or crying. One man was tottering precariously and decided to sit on the floor in the middle of the walkway.

"Sit on a chair, please, sir," the staff member behind the desk yelled. "No, not on the floor. On a chair, please!"

Her words fell on the deaf ears of a drug-addled man whose least concern in the world was where he was sitting.

Within a few minutes, a security guard who had been looking at Ide came over and said, "You are on the wrong line."

He then took her to the correct line and waited with her to tell the intake person what she needed. Later, Ide realised there wasn't a line where she had been standing. She would have been standing on it a long time, getting nowhere.

Once Ide was inside the Trauma Unit, amidst the chaos, she was in awe of how the whole thing worked. Innumerable staff walked up and down the corridors, wearing at least twelve uniforms she had seen. Waldmeer Hospital had three. You were either a doctor, a nurse, or everything else put together under one nondescript, grey uniform everyone hated.

Despite the number of staff and the complexity of what was happening, they all seemed to know what they were doing and, further, what each other was supposed to be doing. Ide thought it looked like an invisible conductor was orchestrating them. If Christopher needed to be moved, five would suddenly appear from nowhere to help.

She didn't tell any of them that she was a nurse. Right now, she didn't feel like a professional. She was a worried mother and wanted to be treated as such.

At one point, a nurse was filling out a form and asked Ide her name as Christopher's next of kin. The reminder that she was a person with a name (and corresponding human emotions) made Ide cry so that she couldn't get her name out. The nurse stopped talking and looked at her with concern. Everyone in the room seemed to sense a problem, stopped what they were doing, and stared at Ide and the nurse.

Get it together, Ide scolded herself. *You know what your name and phone number are.*

She answered the questions in an unsteady but functional voice, and everyone decided the moment was over and returned to their tasks.

"I think you are all wonderful," Ide said numerous times to whichever staff member was helping them.

"We do our job to hear things like that," replied one nurse.

It struck Ide how different all the staff members were in personality. Some were kind and loving. The nurse who initially took her to Christopher had such beautiful, compassionate eyes that Ide momentarily wondered if she was an angel. Some were extremely good at their jobs and did their best to ensure the medical procedures were done well. Some were funny.

To be funny in a Trauma Unit is a special gift, thought Ide.

Some were cranky, but even they were helpful to Ide and Christopher in their own way. A girl about twenty fluttered in and out of their section, tidying everything up.

"You are like the mother fixing up the bedroom," said Ide.

The girl laughed and said, "Yes, I can't stand the room being messy."

The mess kept reappearing, and so did she.

As Ide waited for Christopher to return from his operation in the early morning hours, she thought how wonderful and rewarding it is when people follow their calling and do their job well for the genuine benefit of others. Her calling to nursing had been reaffirmed and strengthened. At a time when she depended on the goodwill and skill of other people, she felt acutely grateful to everyone, everywhere, who does their best by giving what they have to offer, no matter what issues they are facing in their own lives.

IN THE AIR

CHAPTER 59
FOREST ROYALTY

In Waldmeer:

Amira looked out her kitchen window at the magnificent magnolia tree in her front garden. It had been the usher of spring with its graceful, pink petals since her parents planted it forty years ago.

Back then, most of the houses in Waldmeer had lovely, loved gardens with flowering trees and shrubs, delightful bulbs, and colourful annuals. As so many places in Waldmeer were now holiday houses, the original gardens were disappearing. Amira's father, Lenny, would talk about the new gardens with contempt.

"That's not a real garden," he would say as he pointed disparagingly to the en masse, clinical plantings and stretches of cement, tiles, and stones.

"They are soulless places for the heartless."

He took it as personally offensive when the gardens of his long-time friends were sold, along with their accompanying houses, and "improved and updated" for the new occupants with busy lives in the city. He would mumble to himself and go out into his garden until he felt better.

When the magnolia blossomed with fragrant majesty each year, he said, "You go through a dull winter when there's nothin' much flowering. It all looks pretty ordinary, and then the magnolia comes out, and you know that spring is in the air. It's the kinda thing that makes a fella glad to be alive."

Not only was spring in the air, but so was love. Mullum-Mullum's wedge-tailed eagle, Aquilla, had been visiting the magnolia tree and glancing into Amira's kitchen window.

The king of the forest, thought Amira, *perched on the queen of the forest.*

Magnolias are often referred to as *the queen of the forest.*

On one visit, Amira noticed another wedge-tailed eagle at the forest's edge. Aquilla and his mate often preened each other and sat together. Other times, they performed dramatic aerobatic flights.

Sometimes, Aquilla dived down at breakneck speed towards his partner. As he pulled out of his dive and remained a few feet above her, she would turn over and fly upside down, stretching her talons towards him. This could be followed by a series of loop-the-loops.

They started to build a nest in the fork of the tallest tree, adding sticks and leaves to the deep, wide creation every day. Amira could see it from her window and watched with delighted anticipation.

CHAPTER 60
PAYOUT

"The car insurance company has let me know what the payout is for my car," said Amira to Teresa on the phone.

The car was a write-off after Amira's accident.

"Great," said Teresa. "You need another car or you can't get into Darnall to help with the shop."

"Yes, well, you may be waiting a while," said Amira.

She had inherited the car from her Dad several years ago. It was old even when he had been driving it.

"I get the grand total of $500," said Amira. "And I think the guy thought that was being generous."

"Oh," said Teresa.

"You know," said Amira thoughtfully, "I don't think you need me at Handspun anymore. It is going in a different direction from when we had it as the Curiosity Shop, and you have Bryan and Clarice's help."

Amira had decided that she wouldn't get another car. She was happy to be around Waldmeer and felt her travelling back and forth to Darnall had done its dash.

The new term at the college would start soon, and Gabriel was reducing his teaching days to take up a business opportunity his long-term friend, Bridgette, had offered him.

Grace and Thomas's business was slowly but surely growing, as were Thomas and Grace. Now that Grace knew how to get into Advaitaguru's meetings, she could go there on her own whenever she wished, so long as the meetings were still running.

"I will help in your Waldmeer bookshop," said Amira.

"I would like to send young Dayne into Handspun to help occasionally," she added.

"Why?" asked Teresa. "He's a lovely boy, but he's not arty."

"Yes, I know," said Amira, "but I want him to go in when Rachael is there."

Teresa laughed and said, "Are you matchmaking?"

She was about to say something about not meddling, but remembered that Amira had set her relationship with Bryan in motion.

"Isn't Rachael a bit too cool for Dayne?" said Teresa.

It was true that the talented weaver wasn't lacking male interest.

"She may feel that she is," said Amira, "but Dayne has a lot of maturity and sensitivity. If Rachael listens to her higher self, I think she will see in Dayne someone who would love her and not use her. It's a much better payout."

CHAPTER 61
ROYALTY OF EMOTION

A s Amira passed the Op Shop, her eyes were drawn to a folded rug in the corner.

"I haven't put it out yet," said the shop manager. "It needs a clean and has a hole in one corner."

Amira ran her hand over it.

"Beautiful," she said.

Turning to the shop manager, she asked, "If I buy it, will one of the men be able to drop it off for me, as I don't have a car anymore?"

"Sure, love," said the manager. "I'll get my husband to take it up the hill for you."

After delivery, Amira dragged it into her back garden and spread it over some rocks. She felt that it needed sunlight and fresh air. She could tell the rug was special, but had no idea that it was the one Herat had given Thomas at the Afghan Light. Herat told Thomas that it was specially chosen for him because it had "undying love and healing" in it.

After Kathleen's passing, Thomas couldn't bear to look at

the rug. When he packed up his belongings for the move to Darnall, he donated it to the Op Shop, telling himself there would be no room in a small apartment for a large rug.

The sun reached from behind a cloud and lit up the rug. Part of the weaving was a different shade from the rest. On closer inspection, Amira could see that it was a word.

I wonder what it means, thought Amira.

Once the rug was in her lounge room, she noticed that the word had disappeared into the rest of the weaving.

How peculiar, she thought. *The word can only be seen in direct sunlight.*

She looked up as a car drove into her driveway. It was Gabriel.

"Beautiful day," said Gabriel, kissing Amira hello. "I've come to get my art stuff from the bungalow. It's ages since I've done any real art, and I need to start again."

"Bungalow?" said Amira, panicked at the idea of him going to the bungalow.

She had not forgotten Great Aunt Evanora's threat. After depositing the Curiosity Shop boxes into the bungalow, she hadn't been in it again. She didn't know if the sisters were visiting in spirit form.

"Yes, bungalow," repeated Gabriel.

"Ah...no," said Amira.

"What are you talking about?" said Gabriel, who had walked around her and down the path.

Again, the sun reached from behind a cloud and lit up the path behind Gabriel. Amira saw someone she had not seen for a long time. It was Gabriel's angel, who always said, "Be patient. He doesn't know what he is doing."

Upon seeing the comforting sight of the angel, she relaxed and felt that other beings were watching over him.

Once Gabriel got into the bungalow and closed the door, he sat down and looked around. His bed was still on its side against the wall where he had moved it the night the roof leaked.

He smiled at the memory of the little girls offering for him to sleep in the house. That was the beginning of his staying in Amira's house.

The bucket was still under the leak. The leak had never been repaired, although he had promised to find out how to do it.

He looked at his easel and remembered painting the best piece he had ever done.

He walked to the window and saw that the garden was tranquil and peaceful. So, he went outside and lay on the grass.

Peace, he thought, *You are king of all the feelings—royalty of emotion.*

A great bird of prey watched him with calm, benevolent interest.

PART III
THE INNER CIRCLE

BORDERFIRMA MOUNTAINS

ODIN OF THE
GREAT VALLEY

CHAPTER 62
TREE HOUSE

n the Borderfirma Mountains (inter-dimensional):
I The boys lay on the wooden floor of the tree house and gazed up into the moving leaves. It was a grand tree house with three stories, a flag at the top, and lights that came on every evening. It was fit for a king, which was just as well because the boys were royal.

Malik was fourteen. He looked over the palace roof into the Borderfirma Mountains. This land belonged to his mother, and the surrounding Borderfirma lands belonged to her siblings. The Borderfirma lands—the Inner Circle.

"It's spring," said Malik. "Odin should be coming to get us soon."

Odin had always been their primary protector. He was huge and powerful, but also funny and a child at heart, which is why the boys enjoyed his company so much.

He lived in the Great Valley in his mother's cottage and had many duties beyond the children. His father had been killed when he was young, and from that time, he had set himself to become strong enough to protect all he loved. In time, he became custodian of the royal children.

As he did not live in the palace, some of his trusted warriors assisted in their care.

"And Mummy should be back soon," said the younger of the two boys.

At eleven, Aristotle felt his mother's absences keenly. It wasn't only because of his age. Malik was more resilient and robust than his younger brother. Aristotle was sensitive to everything around him. He listened to the animals, felt the winds changing, and generally felt much more in his soul than many adults.

"She's only been away a month this time," said Malik.

He was used to his mother's coming and going.

He looked at Aristotle's sweet face and added sympathetically, "Don't worry, buddy. I'm sure she'll be back soon."

Aristotle looked at Malik with admiration and trust. He wished he were as strong as his big brother. He was sure that Malik must be almost as invincible as Odin. The boys' sister was hurriedly walking across the lawn towards them.

"I have wonderful news," she called to them. "Nanny told me that mother will be back in the next few days."

At twenty, Bethany was not much more than a girl, but she already had her own baby. Seeing the boys, the baby squealed with delight and struggled to escape her mother's arms. Bethany only weighed as much as Aristotle. She had trouble holding onto her flailing baby.

"Come down, boys," said Bethany. "I can't hold onto Lentilly for much longer."

"Pass Lentil up to us," said Malik.

Bethany sighed. Ever since she named her baby Lentilly,

Malik had been calling her Lentil. Much to her annoyance, everyone else thought it was such a good name that they also called her Lentil, although, to Bethany's face, they did make an effort to remember her baby's real name. The boys made no such effort.

Not wanting to insult the boys' child-minding ability (but certainly not willing to let Lentilly play at the top of a giant tree with two teenage boys), Bethany was about to entice the boys closer to the ground when Malik pointed beyond the palace gates.

"Look," he yelled. "It's Odin."

Both boys bolted down the tree at breakneck speed, ran to Odin, and jumped all over him. Odin wrestled them with an earnest face as if his life depended on it, and then, when he thought they had had enough, he said that he was hungry and they should all go inside.

The following day, all five of them—Malik, Aristotle, Bethany, baby Lentil, and Odin—set out for Odin's cottage in the Great Valley of the Borderfirma Mountains.

The royal children were usually surrounded by protectors and a loving band of relatives who doted on them. Nanny was the main one. She didn't dote. She was tough and said the children were indulged far too often. She also said that there were many more bad ways for royal children to grow up than good ones and that no grandchild of hers would become a lazy, self-centred adult, not knowing their responsibilities in life. She was tough, but she loved them with a passion. It was rare for the children to set off with only one carer, but Odin was worth an army.

Being relieved at the prospect of getting away from the palace entourage for a while, Bethany insisted to her grandmother, "We'll be fine. Odin and I will look after Lentilly and the boys. Once we are there, we will have Odin's mother. She's as powerful as Odin in her own way."

CHAPTER 63
CHESTER

INTER-DIMENSIONAL

Amira could smell the sweet spring grass. She stretched out her arms and opened her eyes. The sun was warm and soft on her face. Chester licked her. He was Odin's cat.

"We are so glad you have returned, Lady Faith," said Chester.

Amira sat up and looked around. She was in the field beyond Odin and his mother's cottage.

When she was in the Borderfirma Mountains, she remembered her inter-dimensional lives. However, she had no recollection of Borderfirma while on Earth. She had been told it was best that way.

"How are the children?" she asked expectantly.

"They are perfectly fine," said Chester reassuringly, "and very excited to be coming to the Great Valley."

"Has Lentilly grown much?"

"Oh yes," said Chester. "You will be surprised how much she has grown. And she says words now."

He said it so proudly, she wondered if Chester had taught her the words.

"How is Aristotle?" asked Lady Faith.

"He will be glad to see you," said Chester tactfully.

"How long have I been gone this time?" asked Lady Faith. Time was different in Borderfirma.

"A month," said Chester. "It hasn't been too long."

She stood up, shook off her clothes, and said, "I'd better get changed into something more appropriate."

Odin's mother, Nina, sensed Lady Faith's arrival and ran to her with outstretched arms. At least, she ran as fast as an older, overweight lady could run. Nina had long, grey, plaited hair. It was the wrong hairstyle for a woman her age, but Lady Faith thought it was perfect. Her skirt reached her ankles. Her sweater was almost as long. Both were dirty from outside work.

"You look as wonderful as ever," said Lady Faith.

"The children arrive tomorrow morning," said Nina.

That night, as Lady Faith lay peacefully in bed, listening to the many night noises, she thought of the children's father, Zufar. Zufar and Amira had been lifelong mates eons ago. When Amira was twenty-two and living in Charlie's shed in the back hills of Waldmeer, Milyaket had taken her to the Vastandamine Forest to meet with Zufar before he went to a distant dimension. Now that she was in the Borderfirma Mountains, she could recall three other important occasions when Amira, or, more precisely, Lady Faith, reconnected with Zufar.

Lady Faith had always wanted children. However, she was conscious of her responsibilities in Borderfirma and the other dimensions. As a young adult, she sent a request to the Homeland Advisors about the matter. They responded with the following letter.

> Dear Lady Faith,
>
> We are aware of your desires and want you to be happy. We have chosen a suitable father worthy of royal children. However, we must warn you not to get attached to him. Over the years, he will come to you three times to father three children. He will not be able to return at other times. You must also be willing to share the raising of your children with other people, as your responsibilities will not allow you to be a full-time mother. However, the children will be in good hands with your mother, Odin, and Nina. If this is acceptable to you, then expect your visitor soon.
>
> The Advisors, The Homeland

Indeed, it was very acceptable to young Lady Faith, and her special visitor appeared as they said he would. That was about twenty years ago. Nine months later, Bethany was born.

LOWLANDS

CHAPTER 64
TENSION

ON EARTH

In Waldmeer:

"Thank God," said Ide as she lay on the floor of her dear, peaceful lounge room. "No more hospital visits."

She had returned from the city for the last of Christopher's visits to the surgeon after his broken leg.

"No more fighting the city traffic," continued Ide in singsong fashion. "No more crazy hospital. No more graphic YouTube videos."

"What do you mean?" asked Salt.

Ide laughed.

"Every time we saw the surgeon, he thought of another superstar sportsman who similarly broke their leg—skiers, footballers, hockey players, wrestlers, and martial artists. It was all captured on video and then posted on YouTube in slow motion."

Salt understood Ide's reluctance for Christopher to

watch repeats of dramatic leg injuries while he was trying to heal his massive injury.

"Why didn't you stop it?" he asked.

"I would have," said Ide, who would not have been shy in speaking up if she thought something was injuring her son.

"But before I had an opportunity to, I noticed a sparkle in Christopher's eyes."

With each visit and video, Christopher seemed to be gaining a badge of honour that read,

This happened to me too,
and I survived and thrived.

"The first time the surgeon mentioned the videos," said Ide, "I turned to him to see what the heck he was doing, but he didn't even glance at me. He spoke to Christopher as a man, with a man's injury, to be beaten in the 'secret' way that men fix things. So, I left them to their secret ways because I wanted my son to get better and not be psychologically affected by the whole event."

"Now that it's over," said Ide, stretching her wound-up body, "I think all the stress has accumulated in my neck and shoulders."

"Come," said Salt. "Sit up here. I will help."

Both Christopher and Ide had benefited from Salt's magic hands. He was not like the Chinese masseurs that Ide occasionally visited in Darnall. They were great, but Salt was magic. He ran his hand softly over her spine until he found something needing attention. He didn't knead it like the Darnall masseurs. He touched it firmly and slowly until it succumbed to his knowing fingers.

This was the third time that Salt had touched Ide this

way, and today she totally relaxed. She thought that it must be the most relaxing thing in the world. You couldn't pay for it.

Towards the end of the massage, Ide noticed an odd feeling inside her, a tension.

That's strange, thought Ide. *Why am I tensing up?*

She didn't want Salt to notice, but, of course, he did.

"That's enough," said Salt and stopped.

After a while, she recognised it. It was the flickering fire of sexual interest, and it surprised her. She hadn't felt anything like that since Farkas.

Don't be ridiculous, Ide told herself. *Salt isn't like that.*

Still, she couldn't quite get the thought out of her mind.

CHAPTER 65
FINALLY

I n the Leleks:

"Finally, you have come," said Erdo, who was not bothering to soften his exasperation. "How long has it taken you, Gabriel? Didn't Charlie first tell you about me more than ten years ago? And how many times has Amira spoken of me?"

Gabriel was taken aback by Erdo's abrupt manner.

Isn't he supposed to be a spiritual teacher? thought Gabriel disapprovingly.

He wanted to make it clear to Erdo that he wasn't there as one of his budding students. He came because he couldn't find Amira. That was all. He didn't need anything else.

GABRIEL HAD BEEN RINGING Amira for the past week. He initially wanted to ask if she had seen some missing art brushes. However, he became concerned after she didn't return his calls or messages.

He decided to go to Waldmeer, look for the brushes, and see if Amira was in the house. He rang from her garden. No reply. More worrying was that he could hear her phone ringing inside the house.

Breaking in seemed the best solution. He wouldn't have to break anything because the back windows were generally unlocked.

She wasn't in the house. It crossed his mind that maybe he should go to the police and report a missing person. Somehow, that was a little too dramatic.

Knowing Amira, he thought, *she could be somewhere odd or having a non-contactable retreat somewhere.*

Remembering Erdo, the forest mystic, he thought, *He probably knows where she is.*

It was a pristine, clear day, so he headed into the forest for a drive.

"LOOK," said Gabriel in a deliberately patient voice, "I haven't come to you as a student...."

"Then you are trespassing," said Erdo, turning to leave and pointing to the bridge for Gabriel to go.

Oh my God, thought Gabriel, *he is the rudest person ever.*

He bit his tongue and asked Erdo if he knew where Amira was. Erdo pointed to the lake and left. An image formed on the surface of the lake.

> Amira was walking in a mist. There were many ravenous crevices beneath the ground. Before every step, she stopped and closed her eyes. She then continued forward or took a different direction.

Gabriel looked up into the towering trees surrounding the lake, content in their serene environment, and wondered what the image meant. When he returned his gaze to the lake, the image was gone.

I imagine things, he thought. *It's this place.*

Being none the wiser about Amira's whereabouts but telling himself that she must be alright or Erdo would be doing something about it, he crossed back over the walking bridge. He gladly jumped into his car and headed for the city —partially relieved and totally confused.

CHAPTER 66
LADY OF THE NIGHT

INTER-DIMENSIONAL

ack in the Borderfirma Mountains:

B As Odin was travelling with the children, he had to slow his pace. There was no road into the Great Valley, only a walking track. On his own, he could have reached the cottage by the end of the day. However, with the children, they needed to stop overnight.

They stayed in the forest home of one of his warriors. All bunked down on the floor, they had plenty of blankets and a few mattresses to share. It was cosy.

After a long day of travelling, everyone went to sleep instantly. Baby Lentil had fallen asleep in her mother's arms hours ago. Odin carried her most of the way as she was too heavy for everyone else.

After a few hours, Aristotle woke to a deeply sleeping household. He could hear a strange but interesting noise outside. At first, it sounded like the trees talking—he was used to the trees talking. Then he heard the low sound of an animal getting closer. It seemed to be calling his name.

Aristotle, Aristotle.
Come outside. Come outside.

Eventually, he got up and went to see what the sound was. The glowing moon lit the forest's edge, and he saw a black cat moving stealthily between the trees.

"Come with me," said the cat. "I have something important to show you."

The trees were speaking more urgently now, but Aristotle couldn't hear them. He could only hear the cat.

It was almost morning.

Odin dreamed that his cat, Chester, was calling, *Get up.* *Something has happened.*

He sat bolt upright and counted the children.

Thank God, Lentil is at Bethany's side, he thought. *She hasn't crawled off somewhere dangerous. Malik is snoring. But where is Aristotle?*

He ran outside and listened to the trees.

Evanora came and took him away, whispered the trees. *She came in her cat form and took him back to the Borderfirma Lowlands.*

"It's not Aristotle that she wants," said Odin.

No, Master, replied the trees. *It is Lady Faith. Evanora wants Lady Faith to go to the Lowlands in search of Aristotle.*

Lady Faith had four sisters, each ruling a section of Borderfirma—Pearl, Melba, Evanora, and Rose.

Odin and the children hurriedly packed up and left.

"I don't want Mother to go to the Lowlands," said Bethany quietly to Odin.

"Don't you worry," said Odin. "Your mother has angels walking with her. They see things differently."

CHAPTER 67
DREAMING

After consultation with Nina, Lady Faith set out for the Borderfirma Lowlands. She took Odin with her as far as the border between the two lands.

"I must leave you now," said Lady Faith. "I cannot take reinforcement. It is not that sort of a journey."

The exit sign of the Borderfirma Mountains read,

> *Thank you for visiting us.*
> *If you must dream a dream,*
> *at least make it a happy one.*

The entrance sign of the Borderfirma Lowlands only had an image. It was two snakes attacking each other. A king cobra was biting a python, and the python was constricting the king cobra. The cobra died of constriction, and the python died of venom.

Nothing particularly happy about that, thought Lady Faith as she ventured into her sister's territory.

An hour into the Lowlands, a mist moved in like a fugitive. Lady Faith could see very little and sensed extreme danger.

Every step, she paused, withdrew to the inner sanctuary, and asked herself, *Does this feel right?* Her answer came in the form of peace or tension. If she felt tension, she stepped a different way. If she felt peace, she kept going forward.

Dangerous? Yes, but she had her reason for being there.

Lady Faith repeated to herself,

If you must dream a dream,
at least make it a happy one.

CONTRACT

CHAPTER 68
BEING WATCHED

ON EARTH

In *Waldmeer:*

Another week had passed. Still no word from Amira. Gabriel drove to Waldmeer again.

As he entered the bungalow, he had the uneasy feeling of being watched. He looked at the stacked boxes from the Darnall Curiosity Shop.

I don't know why Amira has to keep all this junk from her great-aunts, he thought.

He moved closer to the stack and was about to open one of the boxes when he heard a loud call from the forest. Walking to the door, he spotted two eagles in a nearby tree, gazing at him.

"Who are you?" asked a woman at Amira's back door.

"Who are you?" asked Gabriel in surprise.

The woman was about forty, with dark, curly hair and the focused, intelligent eyes of a driven, uncompromising person.

"My name is Eve," said the woman. "I am the grand-daughter of Amira's Great Aunt Evanora."

Although Amira had never mentioned Eve, Gabriel felt he should be friendly. He instantly disliked her.

"I'm Gabriel," he said. "I sometimes use the bungalow. Where is Amira?"

"She's not coming back," said Eve emotionlessly. "I am the new owner of the house."

She waved a piece of paper at Gabriel.

"And by the way," continued Eve, "you are no longer welcome in the bungalow."

She opened the back door and said over her shoulder, "Have a good day."

CHAPTER 69
CURRENCY

INTER-DIMENSIONAL

n the Borderfirma Lowlands:

I Although Lady Faith did not know where Aristotle was in the Lowlands, she knew that Evanora would come to her sooner or later.

"Hello, Faith," said Evanora.

"Hello, Lady Evanora," said Lady Faith.

"Let's not chit-chat," said Evanora. "You want your son back. There is a price."

"Yes, I am here," said Lady Faith, implying that she would pay whatever the price was. "What is it that you want? My life for his?"

"Oh no," laughed Evanora. "I want something much more valuable than your life. I want your ability to manifest on Earth in human form."

Although Evanora could travel to Earth in spirit form, unlike Lady Faith, she could not appear there in human form. Years ago, she used her one Earth life as Great Aunt Evanora.

"I see," said Lady Faith quietly.

It was a high price.

"I can visit many dimensions," said Lady Faith tactfully. "Earth is of no particular value."

Evanora snarled.

"Earth," she demanded. "Earth is what I want."

"As you wish," said Lady Faith. "My ability to travel to Earth, as a human, in exchange for my son."

She added, "I want him first."

Evanora pointed behind her. Aristotle was sitting, distressed but unharmed, on a hill of large, flat rocks. Lady Faith ran to him and pulled him to her.

"You have your precious boy," said Evanora. "Now give me Earth."

Lady Faith closed her eyes, touched her forehead lightly, and then touched Evanora's forehead. Evanora smiled and turned to leave.

"Oh, one more thing," said Evanora. "Sign this."

It was a contract of sale for Amira's Waldmeer home.

"You won't need it anymore, but I will," said Evanora.

Lady Faith signed the piece of paper.

"Earth people think they own things by signing papers," said Evanora. "Stupid, I know, but that's what they do."

And with that, her path to Earth was secured—under the name Eve, now at Amira's back door, telling Gabriel he was no longer welcome.

~

LADY FAITH and Aristotle found themselves at the intersection of the Borderfirma Lowlands and the Borderfirma Mountains.

"We are in home territory," said Lady Faith. "Safe and sound."

"But Mummy," said Aristotle, "you gave away your power to return to Earth."

"Well then," said Lady Faith brightly, "we can all have a wonderful time together with Odin and Nina in the Great Valley."

"Let's hurry home before it gets dark," said Odin, who was at the edge of the forest where he had been waiting for them. "Nina will have our dinner cooking, and we don't want to miss that."

CHAPTER 70
CHERISH

ON EARTH

In Waldmeer:

Gabriel stood outside Amira's garden gate, wondering what to do. A car pulled up behind him.

"Do you know where Amira is?" asked Farkas through the open car window. "I haven't seen her in weeks."

"No," said Gabriel. "Apparently, she sold her house to her cousin."

"That dark-haired woman?" asked Farkas.

He had seen the new resident a few times over the last few days and also disliked her.

"I went to Erdo," said Gabriel, "but he wasn't much help."

After a thoughtful pause, Farkas said, "I'll go see him. I used to work for him. He'll talk to me, I think."

On the way to Erdo, Farkas couldn't help feeling a sense of satisfaction that Gabriel and Amira hadn't quite worked out together. He knew he shouldn't feel like that, but he did.

Erdo was waiting for Farkas at the lake. For all of Farkas's issues, Erdo was generally not harsh with him. He knew the effort it took for Farkas to come to him. That had a lot of karmic merit. He also did not want to sabotage Farkas's progress by upsetting him unnecessarily. He saved that for when it was needed.

"She has gone away," said Erdo. "I'm sorry. As I understand, she is safe. I do not know if she will be returning. As she is safe and there is nothing else we can do about it, I suggest we get on with life and concentrate on our mental practices."

It wasn't Erdo who needed the mental practice, but he included himself to entice Farkas into seeing life as an opportunity to practise things that would make him happier.

"Whenever you feel a spark of love or goodwill towards another person, feed it so it will grow," said Erdo.

"It is not about finding the right person. People are not that right," he laughed. "Even if they start right, we soon have a litany of complaints. The only answer is to be the right person ourselves."

Erdo stretched towards the sky as if drawing sunlight and pure forest air into his ageless body.

"And when it does work," he continued, "don't be waving contracts, written or invisible, in front of people. Love that controls is not love."

CROSSING

CHAPTER 71
SEPARATION AND LOVE

In Waldmeer:

Spring was well underway in Waldmeer, and Farkas decided to do some weeding in the garden. Recently, whenever he was in the back garden, he noticed that strange thoughts seemed to filter to the forefront of his mind. He didn't know why or where they came from. One of those thoughts was,

You have far more connection than you are even vaguely aware of. You will not lose the love that is yours.

The thought kept repeating itself. He couldn't say that it was unwelcome, but nor could he say that he understood it (not that the thought seemed to mind whether he understood it or not). It spoke in a relaxed, unhurried way as if passing the time of day. Farkas wondered what exactly he was connected to, what love was his, and (if he couldn't lose it) in what form it was kept.

One morning, as he weeded, he noticed a plant in the corner that he had never seen before. After discovering it, he checked on its progress frequently and took special care of it.

For some odd reason, he felt more settled and less worried whenever he was near it.

He would sit for longer than usual and enjoy the garden and the day—the smell of the grass, the sound of the birds, the blue of the sky, the softness of the breeze, the grandness of the trees.

He became very still, and his breathing deepened.

There was a contented feeling inside his body.

Amira was back!

Although she could no longer travel from the Inner Circle to Waldmeer as a human, she still had her ability to travel inter-dimensionally as a spirit. So, she did just that.

CHAPTER 72
FORKING AROUND

I*n Waldmeer:*

Gabriel didn't want his few bits of furniture left in Amira's bungalow now that it belonged to someone else. They weren't worth anything, and it would have been more practical to forget about them, but he wasn't ready to forget about anything.

He politely knocked on the house door to inform Eve that he was there, but, to his relief, there was no answer.

Once inside the bungalow, Gabriel's eyes were drawn to the Darnall Curiosity Shop boxes that belonged to Amira's great-aunts.

He opened one of them.

He didn't hear the eagles urgently calling to him from the forest.

Suddenly feeling very tired, he sat on his old mattress, which was lying on the floor.

~

INTER-DIMENSIONAL

IN THE INTER-DIMENSIONAL BORDERFIRMA:

Gabriel found himself walking along a quiet road in unfamiliar countryside. It was the road leading to the inter-section of the Borderfirma Mountains and the Borderfirma Lowlands.

In the distance, he could see that the road divided into two. He wondered which road he should take, but realised he didn't know where he was going.

Never mind, he thought, *it's only a dream. I can wake up whenever I want to.*

He could hear the faint sound of a voice up ahead. Straining to listen, he heard,

Think not you can return on the path that leads to the
fork.
Taken once, it disappears as the choice lies ahead.
Both roads will lead to somewhere but one will be to
nowhere.

Once Gabriel reached the fork, he couldn't decide which way to go. He stood there a long time. Every time he took a few steps down one road, he felt dissatisfied. Afraid he was going the wrong way, he returned to the fork.

"The worst place is at the fork," said the voice.

Gabriel turned to see a man with penetrating, grey eyes. It was Mullum-Mullum.

"You can't keep going the same direction as you came," said Mullum-Mullum. "You have to choose one or the other path. Whatever the choice, at least, it is movement."

Mullum-Mullum smiled slightly and said, "Otherwise, you are just forking around, getting nowhere."

Gabriel looked at the stranger to see if he had heard him correctly, but Mullum-Mullum was walking back into the trees.

In exasperation, he chose one path. Before long, he came upon a sign with two snakes. He looked at it and felt afraid. He returned to the fork and took the other way. It, too, had a sign after a while. It said something about dreaming a happy dream.

Seeing as I'm already dreaming, Gabriel thought, *I'd prefer it to be a good one, so I will keep going this way.*

SNAKES AND BITCHES

CHAPTER 73
INDRA

Although the Borderfirma Mountains covered a vast area, Lady Faith's palace stood at the edge of the Lowlands, separated only by the Great Valley. That is why Odin and Nina lived there.

This is a very long dream, thought Gabriel, as he pushed on through the Great Valley after choosing his path at the fork.

There were no more decisions to be made about which way to go because there was only one road through the Great Valley. By now, Gabriel suspected there was more to his journey than a dream. For one thing, he was starving. As he felt he had no hope of knowing what to do if it wasn't a dream, he kept acting on the premise that it was.

Quite a way into the Valley, he came to a river and spotted a boy and a girl, about eleven years old, playing on the banks.

Thank God, thought Gabriel, *civilisation.*

He was about to call to the children when he noticed that

the girl had two cobras around her neck. He panicked and thought he would have to do something to save her. Then, he noticed that she wasn't at all worried about them. She was playing with them. If they got snitchy and snapped at her or each other, she hit them and told them to behave. They didn't behave. They were snakes.

The boy saw Gabriel and called to him in a friendly way. Gabriel immediately liked the child.

"Hello," said the boy. "I'm Aristotle, and this is my friend, Indra. And, oh yes, these are her snakes."

He felt he should include the snakes in case they were the vindictive type.

"Nice to meet you all," said Gabriel.

"Don't worry about them," said Aristotle, pointing to the snakes.

"I wasn't," said Gabriel, but then he felt foolish because the boy had the sort of eyes that could read minds.

"Of course not," said Aristotle in a manner far too grown-up for his age. "Indra is staying with us for a holiday. She lives in the Lowlands with her father. He is the best snake catcher in the land."

"Indra likes snakes," said Aristotle. "They don't like anyone (even her) because they're snakes."

"Why don't you come home with us?" he suggested.

Gabriel eyed the snakes that were now coiling around Indra's waist.

"Don't worry," said Aristotle. "My mother doesn't trust them either. They have to stay in boxes when they're at our house."

"I'm with your mother," said Gabriel.

He added quickly, "I mean your mother's approach to snakes."

Both children laughed, and they all made their way to Nina and Odin's cottage.

CHAPTER 74
ROUND-EARTHER

Lady Faith and Gabriel couldn't have been more surprised and delighted to see each other. It was a loud, happy gathering that evening with many tales being told.

She could see that Gabriel believed he was in a dream. She let him keep that idea.

The next few days were full of laughter, long conversations, and unmarred enjoyment.

Although the children and baby Lentil thought Gabriel was the best thing since sliced bread, and even Nina laughed at all his jokes, Odin was not at all impressed with Gabriel.

"He doesn't have the right respect for her," said Odin one evening to his mother.

"He's too familiar," complained Odin. "I think it's inappropriate. He doesn't even call her by her correct name. He calls her Amira as if she is a common Round-Earther."

"She enjoys him," said Nina. "Let her laugh for a while. She has so many responsibilities."

"It will all end in tears," Odin grumbled. "Mark my words."

CHAPTER 75
NASTY BITCH

On the fourth evening, Gabriel decided to talk about the elephant in the room.

"So, Amira, who is the children's father?" he asked.

"Zufar," said Lady Faith.

She explained, as briefly as possible, about Zufar's background, esteemed reputation, and the Advisor's decision that he would be a suitable father of the royal children.

"Where is he now?" asked Gabriel.

Seeing Gabriel's concern, Lady Faith said, "Oh, he won't come back. We don't even know where he is. He's somewhere. Doing something good."

"I'm sure he is," said Gabriel tersely.

"He only came," said Lady Faith, "to... er... help with the children..."

"Yeah, I get that," said Gabriel. "A one-night stand."

"Technically, it was a three-night stand," smiled Lady Faith, trying to lighten the atmosphere.

Gabriel turned away.

"What if he does come back?" he said as casually as possible.

"He won't," said Lady Faith.

"How do you know?" said Gabriel.

"He can't," said Lady Faith.

"But what if he does?" persisted Gabriel.

"I don't know," said Lady Faith. "Things are different here."

"I noticed," said Gabriel, feeling like he needed to find out how to wake up.

When Gabriel was hurt, he could turn into a particular version of himself, which was Amira's least favourite Gabriel. It was a cross between a bitchy gay guy and a nasty cool girl. The offspring wasn't pretty.

He sometimes became that character when he was with certain company back in Waldmeer. As Amira didn't keep that company, she generally didn't have to see that behaviour.

The next morning, the less-than-pleasant and less-than-welcome visitor was there in fine form. Odin overheard a few of Gabriel's comments and was busting to intervene. Nina looked at him, as only a mother can, to remind him that Lady Faith could handle it herself.

"You have to learn how to deal with being hurt in a better way," said Lady Faith to Gabriel when they were alone.

"I'm not hurt," said Gabriel. "What would I be hurt about?"

"That's the start of the problem right there," said Lady Faith.

Gabriel looked like there was no way in the world, or any other world, that he would tell someone who hurt him that they had done so.

The next day, Odin, who could no longer restrain himself, said, "Ain't no nasty bitches around here, Gabriel. You'll have to go to the Lowlands with Indra for that."

Indra was packing her few belongings and the snakes to make the trip back home.

"Alright," said Gabriel. "I will."

Odin moaned that he should have kept his mouth shut because now he would have to watch over Gabriel as well as the two children on the way to the border.

However, the long walk through the forest had a calming effect on everyone. The children were peaceful. Gabriel started to forget what had previously seemed so disturbing to him, and Odin synced with the rhythm of his beloved forest.

When they got to the border, Gabriel said there were too many snakes for his liking in the Lowlands and that he would return with Aristotle and Odin to the Great Valley.

Later, Lady Faith and Nina saw Gabriel and Odin talking quietly as they crested the home hill.

"Looks like *the nasty bitch* was left at the border," said Lady Faith.

Nina smiled and said, "Yes, both of them."

DOING OUR BEST

CHAPTER 76
SALT AND IDE

ON EARTH

In Waldmeer:

"What do you think, Ide?" asked Salt.

He was standing in his new massage and healing room, at Vibes Yoga Studio, in Waldmeer.

"I love it. It's beautiful. Just like you," said Ide with a kiss.

Salt didn't need her kisses, but he was happy to have them.

Not long ago, he had asked Ide about the idea of him staying in her house for most of the week. Previously, he had been staying there a few days and spending the rest of the week in the back hills with the Clinker clan.

Ide knew that if she said yes, she was saying yes to a couple relationship. She recalled when Farkas asked if she wanted to buy this house jointly with him. At the time, she had considered everything that could go wrong. As it turned out, some of them did happen. However, most of her fears didn't eventuate, and many wonderful moments came from her and Farkas's time together. One of those moments turned into their child, Lan-Lan.

Her greatest fear had been that the relationship would fall apart.

It did fall apart, thought Ide, *and you know what? We are fine.*

"No one replaces anyone else," said Salt. "Every person is unique. Every relationship is unique."

He walked to the window and continued, "Life is fluid—it moves. It doesn't die—it reforms."

Looking towards the Clinker hills in the distance, and then to the town below, he said, "Each day is new. We can only try to do our best today. It's enough, don't you think? No more is asked. But also, no less."

Nothing more was said about it, and both assumed the agreement had been agreed to.

SRI AND GLORIA came into Salt's new room at the yoga studio to have a look.

"Looks great in here," said Sri. "Where did you get the rug?"

"When I was driving here," said Salt, "I passed Amira's old house, and the new owner had put some furniture and this rug on the nature strip. So, I took it."

Gloria ran her hand over it.

"Gorgeous," she said. "It makes you want to lie on it and float away."

She took Ide's hand, and they both lay on the rug.

Although Gloria and Amira had not worked out as friends, Gloria found Ide a more viable female companion.

In her heart, Gloria knew that the problem with Amira was jealousy, but she couldn't get rid of the feeling. She not only felt jealous, but she felt bad about being jealous. It was easier to avoid her. Besides, Gloria and Ide had the common ground of toddler boys.

The toddlers were playing with the yoga props in the main room. They rolled and unrolled the mats with endless amusement, piled the yoga blocks to make castles, knocked them over with equal delight, pushed the round bolsters along the floor like road rollers, and jumped on the stacked blankets like a trampoline.

"I saw an Arabic word woven into the rug," said Salt. "I wrote it down. Can you read it, Sri?"

Sri spoke several languages—English, Hindi, and Arabic.

Sri looked at the word, لا يموت, and said, "*undy*ing."

CHAPTER 77
ODIN AND MALIK

INTER-DIMENSIONAL

In the *Borderfirma Mountains:*

Today was the last day of Lady Faith and the children's holiday in the Great Valley with Odin and Nina.

"I have an important announcement," said Malik over breakfast.

Everyone looked at Malik and then at Lady Faith, expecting she would already know about the important announcement.

"I don't know anything," said Lady Faith. "Malik is a young man now. He doesn't need to run things past his mother anymore."

"I will not return to the palace tomorrow," Malik said. "I will be staying here to continue my training with Odin."

Over the holidays, Odin and Malik spent a great deal of time training in the forest. Odin gave Malik various-sized pieces of wood as weights. He taught him how to do pull-ups on tree branches, drag big logs, and chop wood for strength and endurance training. Odin also made Malik run along the never-ending forest tracks. He gave him simple stretches so that his rapidly increasing muscle mass would not detract from his speed and flexibility. Malik much preferred the weight training.

One afternoon, he jumped from a tree branch and landed like a fridge smashing into the ground.

"That's odd," said Malik. "I could always jump from great heights without a problem."

"You see," said Odin, "if you keep building muscle and don't include your exercises for suppleness and movement, you will become too slow and heavy. Everything is balance."

After Malik's announcement, everyone rushed to him with congratulations and sadness.

Lady Faith sat still while the fuss was being made. Malik was not her oldest child, but, as it turned out, was the first to leave home. She smiled at him in acknowledgement.

Malik saw the respect in her eyes.

Although he had made his decision independently, he searched for that look on his mother's face.

When he found it, he knew his path had indeed been chosen.

CHAPTER 78
GABRIEL AND ARISTOTLE

Today was also Aristotle's twelfth birthday. In the afternoon, his family gave him a few handmade presents—a little book about forest birds that Bethany had illustrated, a leather bag that Odin and Malik had made from the hides of deceased animals, and a special cake from his mother. The last present was from Nina.

"I must say that this present isn't exactly from me," said Nina. "I don't even know what it is."

She went to her room and brought out a large, flat parcel.

"The last time your father was in these parts," said Nina, "he delivered this parcel to us here in the Great Valley. He said it was for Aristotle's twelfth birthday. That was how we learned you would be born in nine months. The worst part was keeping you a secret."

She passed Aristotle the parcel. Everyone was intensely interested to see what it could be.

"An old picture frame," said Aristotle, trying not to show his disappointment.

"With no picture in it," said Malik.

The two boys looked at each other, unsure of what to make of their father's gesture.

"There is something written on the back," said Nina.

I want my children to remember that the frame does not matter, but the picture does. Make sure that the picture is beautiful. The frame is only there to draw the eyes to the picture.

The two boys again looked at each other blankly.

"There is something else in small print," said Nina.

This frame entitles Aristotle and one adult companion to an Earth visit. It must be used today. Choose your companion wisely. Stand in the frame, and you will find yourself transported.

"Wow," said Bethany. "Earth. What fun. How I would love to visit Earth."

Then a hush set over the group.

The problem was obvious. Aristotle would want to take his mother, and she needed to return to Earth. However, it wasn't Gabriel's choice to be here. Evanora had pulled him to Borderfirma, hoping to entice him to the Lowlands.

"I will take Gabriel," said Aristotle cheerfully, "because he will be more fun than Mum."

His eyes radiated wisdom and kindness. He did not want Gabriel to feel responsible for the choice.

That child, thought Lady Faith, *has too much empathy for a twelve-year-old boy.*

"Hey, I can be fun," said Lady Faith. "If I want to. Sometimes."

Everyone laughed.

Although many things went over Gabriel's head in Borderfirma, he knew what Aristotle was doing. He admired the child. He didn't know what to say. He couldn't offer to stay in Borderfirma instead of Lady Faith because he didn't know what he was doing there. It was all beyond him at this stage.

"I do have a birthday present for you, after all," Gabriel said suddenly. "I will be your personal guide on Earth. It's a good offer."

Later that day, as Gabriel and Aristotle prepared to leave via the frame, Gabriel said, "Ah, there's one small problem, or should I say large problem. Aristotle is skinny. He will fit through the frame, but I am too, ah, big."

"You mean fat," laughed Malik.

"I'll push you through," said Odin.

"Thanks, guys," said Gabriel sarcastically.

"Just stand in it after Aristotle," said Nina. "You will have dematerialised before your belly gets to the frame."

After many goodbyes, Aristotle disappeared through the frame, saying, "Don't be long behind me, Gabriel. I'm scared."

"Don't worry, buddy," said Gabriel. "I'll be right behind you."

Lady Faith put her hand on Gabriel's heart and closed her eyes. She looked at him steadily on opening her eyes again, stepped back, and said, "Look after my boy."

CHAPTER 79
LADY FAITH AND BETHANY

The next morning, Lady Faith, Bethany, baby Lentil, and Odin were ready to set out on their journey to the palace.

"It will just be you and me here tonight, Malik," said Nina. "Aristotle is on an adventure with Gabriel, and your sister has to return to the palace with your mother so she can start learning how to rule the Borderfirma Mountains."

"Ha-ha," said Bethany.

Nina didn't laugh.

"What are you talking about, Nina?" asked Bethany more seriously. "As if I could run Borderfirma. And, anyway, Mum is here."

She suddenly panicked and said, "Right? That's right, isn't it?"

"You are your mother's daughter, aren't you?" said Nina. "You are more than capable."

"Calm down, Bethany," said Lady Faith. "Everything is fine. I'm not going anywhere until you are ready."

"But where?" said Bethany.

"The Inner Circle is not the end of the journey," said Lady Faith. "There is another land. It lies between Border-firma and the higher dimensions. It is a place where all illusions are dismantled. Once there, the pull to higher dimensions is very great."

"What?" said Bethany in distress.

Odin also looked more than a little concerned.

Lady Faith pulled herself back to the here and now and looked at them both.

"Oh, don't worry, you two," she said. "I'm not going yet. And I'm not staying there. They told me I'd be back."

"Come on then," said Odin, satisfied that there was no imminent danger of his world collapsing.

He put his arms around Bethany (who was holding Lentil) and Lady Faith, and said with rather more familiarity than he would normally dare, "I have my three favourite girls. So, I'm a lucky man. Let's get back to the palace. We have had a wonderful holiday, but we have much to do now."

SUMMARY OF WALDMEER SERIES

A multi-generational journey of spiritual awakening, healing, and the spaces between worlds.

Beneath the surface of an idyllic coastal village, unseen forces stir. Waldmeer is a place where the visible and invisible meet—where inter-dimensional realms brush against everyday life, and where emotional truths rise quietly but undeniably.

Told across seven books, the *Waldmeer Series* follows Maria–Amira from the groundedness of her rural home to the doorways into higher realms of perception and spiritual transformation. Around her, those she loves and seeks to help are drawn into their own awakenings, resistances, and reckonings.

Waldmeer moves between ordinary moments and otherworldly initiations. Between earthly love and higher love. Between who we think we are... and what we truly are.

At times tender, at times confronting, these stories unfold in layers—personal, relational, and metaphysical.

ABOUT THE AUTHOR

On the beach at Lorne, Australia (the coastal village Waldmeer is based on).

Donna Goddard is a spiritual author whose work blends clarity, devotion, and metaphysical insight. With more than twenty published books across spiritual nonfiction, fiction, poetry, and children's literature, she writes to uplift consciousness and offer healing through words.

Donna's Facebook author page has over 400,000 followers worldwide, and her YouTube channel has received 4 million views. Her books are read by spiritual seekers globally and are known for their honesty, poetic style, and transformative energy.

Her writing is an offering—to help others awaken their own inner spirit, trust its guidance, and create a life of depth, beauty, and quiet joy.

All links at https://linktr.ee/donnagoddard

Ratings and Reviews

Donna would be grateful for any ratings or reviews.

ALSO BY DONNA GODDARD

Fiction
Waldmeer Series: A Spiritual Fiction Series
Nanima Series: Spiritual Fiction
Enanika Series: Visionary Fiction
Riverland Series (children's fiction 6 to 9 years)
Foxie (children's fiction 7 to 12 years)

Nonfiction
Love and Devotion Series
Sweet Spirit Series
Consciousness Series
Meditation Series
Poetry Series
Love's Longing
Dance: A Spiritual Affair
Writing: A Spiritual Voice